MAKER
OF
DIFFERENCE

Carrie Simon

innovo
PUBLISHING

Published by Innovo Publishing, LLC
www.innovopublishing.com
1-888-546-2111

Providing Full-Service Publishing Services for Christian Authors, Artists & Ministries:
Books, eBooks, Audiobooks, Music, Film & Courses

MAKER OF DIFFERENCE

Unless otherwise noted, all scripture is taken from the King James Version (KJV)
of the Bible.

Scripture marked "NASB" is taken from the NEW AMERICAN STANDARD
BIBLE®, Copyright © 1960,1962,1963,1968,1971,1972,1973,1975,1977,1995 by
The Lockman Foundation. Used by permission.

Library of Congress Control Number: 2019908117
ISBN: 978-1-61314-512-8

Cover Design & Interior Layout: Innovo Publishing, LLC

Printed in the United States of America
U.S. Printing History
First Edition: 2019

This book is dedicated to family and friends as well as all those who choose to live life to the fullest and be makers of difference. Being courageous in compassion, ever humble, proclaiming Truth to all, they were set apart.

***

We all want to be something, do something, that will leave a trace behind—to say we were here, if only for a moment. That our dreams, hopes, aspirations, and desires had purpose and meaning and were not just for happenstance, but that we made an impact upon others, a lasting legacy within which to live on long after our bodies turned to dust. And regardless of our shortcomings and failures, that we made the world just a little better by our presence in it. Choosing not only to make a difference in this world but to be one as well. To take a stand even when afraid or alone and say, "I will live for something, and I will die for something. My one life will count, it will matter, and it will encourage others to be courageous."

The Girl

L ark wished she could recall every detail of the first day she met him, but she could not, and, try as she might, it really didn't matter in the grander scheme of things. What did matter, however, is how it happened and what was changed for eternity ever after by a few encounters. She, for one, was hardly noteworthy, and yet . . . her amazing story was.

She lived in a quiet and secluded area with enough yard for her to yawn on the porch in her pajamas and not give a second thought about it. A place where you could see your neighbors if you wanted to and listen only if you chose to. Where creaking wooden floors took the place of a train whistle or the clambering of many a person walking groggily to their early morning destinations. Perhaps that's why she was christened her name. Just maybe her doting parents knew, like a bird, she needed space, not confinement. Not constraints, but freedom.

However, this sweet sentiment was only mere speculation and cannot be given more weight than a simple opinion because they were no longer alive to ask. Tragically, her time with them was fleeting, and she had not always appreciated the moments when she had them near her. Both of them enjoyed successful careers and devoted what time they could to her, but, sadly, Lark had chosen so-called friends and mere acquaintances over her parents' offers of companionship more times than she could recall. She ultimately regretted it only when she stood over their grave sites as the eulogies were read.

Now older and wiser, she stared back at her long, brown hair and green eyes and squarely tried to pinpoint what all she inherited from them besides a happy mixture of both their resemblances. The long mirror appeared as if it was playing tricks on her as her eyes bored into the image staring back at her. She studied her thin frame, curious if her mother had stood years ago, doing the very same thing and wondering at the time what she would look like in years to come. Shrugging her shoulders, Lark grew tired of thinking of only sad things, and yet they seemed unavoidable. Too much time to reminisce on things that could not be changed led her to feel even more of a recluse and detached from all the hustle and bustle of useless and unnecessary society/socialistic exercises, such as "going out" or keeping apprised of the latest "fashion trends," neither of which she missed at all. But too much solitude was not so great either, so the new companionship she had with *him*, while surprising, brought a sense of camaraderie for her, even if it was sporadic and short-lived. If anything, it only bolstered that age-old adage that "substance outweighs the sum."

Lark had grown up as a typical precocious child and naive teenager. She maintained good grades in school and still excelled in sports. Her parents had attended the same church for years, and at the tender age of nine, she had given her life to Christ, or so she claimed the time she stood next to the pastor on a random Sunday evening service when she had felt compelled to walk down the aisle to him instead of remaining in her pew. She knew now that it was divine conviction, but at the time, she simply argued that it felt like the right thing to do, never truly realizing what all that meant until much later. Realistically, everyone was elated when she announced her decision, and she enjoyed the attention that ensued.

For a couple of years after, she read her Bible, attended Sunday school, and genuinely wanted to put God and His priorities first. But once she became a teenager, the eloquent words of the pastor began to fade to a distant memory, and a new voice emerged. It was a voice of defiance and resistance, but to her it simply sounded like her own voice. She spent years with this type of mentality. Reasoning in such a simple mind that she was only breaking free from the constraints of complacency and freeing her body and mind from the beast of tradition. Looking back upon that time in her life splattered and slayed by memories of regrettably wasted years and disenchanted friends, it all seemed so foolish.

That was why it did not seem logical to her that He should have chosen her. After what she could only call heavenly intervention, she came to her senses toward the age of twenty-seven and began to glean from her mistakes in order to encourage others to avoid them. However, most of the time, this was met with severe pushback because we are stubborn, hardheaded, and, yes, hard-hearted beings when we are not walking in obedience to God. But even then, she was somewhat ineffective because she wanted to plant one foot in the right direction and the other foot in whatever happened to be the "trend." Dangerous and terribly unwise, but she knew that now. Then, she didn't. She was still blinded, despite her desire to improve. She traveled a lot back then and met many people, some worthy of notation, some she personally felt did not deserve a second glance, but then again, these were the days before enlightenment. Years before she realized just how far God was willing to go for each one of us, to have—or in her case, renew—a deep and abiding relationship with Him.

Once she had completed college, Lark began to devote herself to trying to repair and restore the home that her parents had left her, along with their belongings, as an inheritance. It was what one would call a large manor, set back on approximately fifty acres of land that seemed to loom in the distance and bring a rather "otherworldly" air about the place. It had been in the family for years, passed down with love and honor but in dire need of a plethora of repairs. Each day, through the grief after the loss of her parents, she added another stroke of the paintbrush or another nail to an additional fixture. She tried to manage a smile, realizing that it was with fondness, adoration, and a sense of accomplishment that she lay in bed at night.

For years, this became her life: choosing to only venture out when she needed, and even then just for a very short time. Most of the childhood friends she had known were gone, or if they had stayed in the area, they had married and had children to raise. That was a significant lifestyle difference than her own that left her feeling more and more distant, not because she did not care but because she had lost the commonalities they all once shared. She hated the thought of becoming some creepy old recluse, but when the years began to go by without so much as a whisper in the wind of another companion with which to share her life, she delved further and further into a life that only she knew and enjoyed.

Those who did wave and smile when she needed things from town were always met with mere pleasantries, but nothing more. They left Lark to her privacy, and, despite a few instances when she longed for more, she was glad they didn't push or prod a conversation when she wouldn't have any idea where to begin. It wasn't as if Lark had not been gregarious in her younger days or that she had nothing of importance to say. Rather, it had been so long since she had felt affection or had a meaningful conversation that she was more afraid to extend one than anything else. Even her own voice sounded foreign to her, and her courtesies sounded like mechanical and perfunctory responses more than heartfelt replies.

Sometimes, though, she was perfectly content to be left alone without having to share her own little world with anyone else, but as the years continued to go by and the holidays (especially the holidays) came and went with only memories of her beautiful parents taken too soon, Lark began to drift into a type of sadness that left her crying in more moments than she would like to admit, without anyone around to share it with—or so she thought.

All that time, all those tears, all those words spoken alone in the dark had been heard, were felt, and were not in vain when *he* appeared to shed clarity instead of confusion. Everything she had ever known or thought she did was changed, leaving her to think more clearly and more openly than she had ever dared to. She suddenly was thrust into an opportunity that defied human reasoning and logic, yet it was very real. Leaving an impact she prayed would also dispense a lasting impression upon others' hearts. Searing an image in their minds that would become engraved for all eternity.

You see, there she was, on a typical day when the leaves of the maple trees had begun to change, and the air had become crisp and chilly. She was never too fond of the weather changes. When the warm breezes would turn to a more frigid wind, its effects made her shiver, and she didn't want to get out of her warm bed full of oversized pillows and layers of blankets. She was almost done pulling up the floor of the kitchen and repairing it; she wanted to finish it before the weather got too cold for her to even bother, knowing she would quickly lose interest. She tried to force herself to get up and get started but instead stared out the window, watching a few colorful leaves fall from the trees.

Living alone took discipline because after so many years of not being required to go to a job or feeling the prompting of anyone, it was easy to just sit back and become lethargic over time. For her, forcing herself to move and do things gave her gratification and healing from the grief of being without any family. Lark refused to succumb to some sort of emotional crutch like drugs or overeating to stifle the sting of loneliness and sadness. Imagining her father's stern face disapproving of that type of behavior was enough for her to steer clear of what most had turned to.

Once out of bed, she fumbled to find her favorite comfy slippers and grab an old bathrobe of her father's. It had lost its smell of him over the years, but she knew it would. It still was comfy and, for now, was the closest thing to her without having to walk into one of the large closets to retrieve "real" clothes before morning coffee.

Walking toward the kitchen, she managed to stifle a yawn and placed her hands on the countertop. Admiring some of her remodeling handiwork, she paused for a moment to simply survey the room. How different it had looked when she was younger. Now, sleek lines and large natural slabs of marble took it from outdated and somewhat boring to fresh, open, and modern. The stones gave both an ancient and futuristic design, and Lark liked it. Smiling, her eyes rested on the large, silver canister labeled "Coffee." *Now that will wake me up,* she thought, and began pouring the rich and pungent grounds in the filter of the coffee pot. She had already placed enough water in it the night before but had forgotten the grounds. A step easily rectified as she finished scooping them in, pushed the coffee maker back to its original position, and pressed the start button.

Ahh . . . she could already imagine its smooth taste and warmth. Her mother never cared for it. She had preferred the sweetness of a tea, like Earl Grey. Lark wasn't completely against tea. In fact, she was quite fond of it, but for different reasons. She drank coffee because she enjoyed it. Tea . . . well, that was for when she needed a cure. For upset stomach, peppermint or ginger. Anxiousness or insomnia, chamomile. The list went on and on. Her mother knew of these cures and passed them down to her, as her mother before her, and so on. But for Lark's mother, it had been enjoyment as well and, to Lark's understanding, had never let any coffee pass her lips.

Lost in a string of memories, the beeping sound from the coffee maker instantly jolted her back to reality. So, grabbing a cup from the large cabinets above, she poured herself the coffee and grabbed a small notebook that lay haphazardly on the counter. "Pick me up; tell me your secrets," Lark pretended the book said as she opened its slender cover and stared intently on its blank, intimidating pages. This too had been a gift from her parents. And just as the day she had received it, she tossed it to the side without a moment's notice. She could not figure out how it had gotten in the kitchen. Had she moved something and left it there? She couldn't recall. All she knew was that she was glad to be nice and warm inside, drinking a hot cup of coffee and undeterred by any outside influence.

A few doves flew by as she watched the world of nature move about from the large windows in the kitchen, but these were normal and pleasant distractions. She wasn't necessarily so fond of the oversized windows, but her dear, sweet mother had been; she always wanted more windows. It wasn't so much the thought of the desire for fresh air, mind you, but more akin of her desire for sweet sunshine. Lark used to think it was odd when she was younger, but now she understood. She had debated boarding them up from time to time, especially in light of the fact that she lived alone, but too many changes brought about uneasiness somewhere deep down inside of her. Certain modifications were off-limits because she secretly feared that if she made too many, all the beautiful memories of days long ago would fade away, and the possibility of creating new ones with anyone else was looking mighty bleak.

She continued to sip and daydream. This was usually her time to read the local and regional newspapers, which made her connected in a way and aware of current events. So, making herself a bit more comfortable, she found the latest edition and sat down, her coffee in hand.

The front page featured the local high school and highlights of their football championship game. The team had been victorious, and the front page and subsequent ones were littered with the smiling faces of young teenage boys or coaches. Even if she didn't interact much anymore these days, she still felt a sense of pride for the local team who exhibited such hard work and talent. Even a local 4-H livestock show was featured as each child or teenager beamed with their blue ribbons.

Lark continued to turn the pages until her eyes rooted on a different article that read, "It's been years ago, but we still miss you, Joseph. You were worth more than you knew. Dad, Mom, and Sister." A couple of messages regarding other individuals stating things such as, "Missing you," or, "Happy birthday! You would have been thirty years old," also lined the pages, but only the first one really moved her and touched her heart. The face staring back at her appeared to be a happy teenage boy with unruly hair and a toothy grin. Had he died by an accident? Or was it something else? She didn't really recognize his face, but she still felt overwhelmingly sad.

Continuing to read the rest of the paper, she finished her coffee and stretched out her legs. She needed to get dressed. Tossing her bathrobe across the back of one of the chairs in the kitchen, Lark walked down the long hallway and into her bedroom again, struggling with the monotony.

Lately Lark had not been as clean and organized for some reason. A variety of small piles of clothes lay carelessly around the room, and her unsightly, disheveled bed was full of different-sized pillows and colored blankets. With the recent renovations, she was exhausted as each day drew to a close, and now, looking at the mess that just one person could accumulate in such a short time disgusted her. The entire house needed a good cleaning, and perhaps that should be the priority over the other projects on the agenda.

Putting on a pair of her favorite jeans and a long-sleeved shirt, Lark determined just that. Soon the infusion of caffeine from the coffee aided this desire, and she welcomed the burst of energy. She went from room to room armed with her cleaning supplies and before long was able to sit on the couch in the living room. She was proud that she had accomplished most of her cleaning, and all before trying to decide what she was going to do for dinner. Even the air smelled cleaner.

She got back up from the couch, determined to finish what she had started. It was slow going with certain chores like dusting. Mainly because she dreaded it. That and bathroom cleaning were her least favorites, and yet putting them off for this long made the rooms feel grimy and infectious. Her mother had always kept the house to a meticulous standard. Lark, on the other hand, felt it was pointless with all her renovations to keep sweeping or wiping up dust. She had figured that once all that was over with, she would do some sort of "spring cleaning," and that would be the end of it. But time had lapsed, certain projects were either semi-done or not yet started, and she was neglecting everything else. After a few more hours of intense cleaning, even she was beaming with satisfaction.

"Not too shabby," Lark said to herself as she closed another door off. Whenever she cleaned, she would start from the back of the house and work her way up to the front, which was the living/sitting room and the kitchen. As she cleaned each room, she would shut its door, signaling that she was through and on to the next one. Not only did this help her know what needed to be done next, but it was also a "mental motivator" so she could see what was accomplished and feel productive in her endeavors.

Now almost completed, Lark's second wind was in full force and she was running faster than ever, cleaning with unbridled vigor. Too bad she wasn't always this motivated. But why was the picture of that young boy still in her head? The more she cleaned, the more she thought about him, his eyes, the joy of happiness caught in a brief second on camera. *Why is life like that?* she wondered. *Struggles and hardships on a daily basis, and then, as if a cruel joke has been played, we are snatched away when we are in our happiest moments.* Looking back, she wasn't really sure why she went to grab the newspaper again where she had left it. Nearly everything had been completed except for the slow rumble of the dryer in the laundry room, finishing what was left of the clothes, and she wasn't in any hurry to fold them. Flipping the pages to where she knew the article was, she studied his face once again and instantly wanted to cry. She didn't know why and she couldn't help it; it was the strangest thing. She paused as she wiped her eyes. She thought it might have only reminded her that life itself was fleeting, but for some reason it was more than that. Now in hindsight, she realized that at the very instant she saw his face, she knew she was destined to save him.

She decided on a whim to cut the picture out and place it in her room along with the numerous other photos that were priceless to her. Sensing a strange feeling of familiarity, she placed it nearest her parents' photo frame. He was cute in a teenager way. Too young for her, of course, but definitely cute enough to have a steady girlfriend. She tried as hard as she might to narrow down any part in her life when she may have come into contact with such an individual. She ventured to town very seldom, and he was too young to have attended school with her, nor did his name sound remotely familiar. *Oh well.* Lark's frustration was mounting that she couldn't identify him or understand why her feelings were so strong, so she decided to walk around the property to clear her thoughts.

After putting on a jacket and a pair of tennis shoes, she walked out of the front door and onto the porch. The wind hit her nostrils, and a faint whiff of jasmine filled the air and caused her to close her eyes, recalling how her mother was delighted that it was growing on their property. Lark wondered if jasmine grew in heaven as she stepped off the porch and began walking along the edges of the property. When she was little, she had walked it in that same fashion with her father who would let her pretend to be surveying it for anything that needed to be done. She didn't believe that he had any formal training in horticulture, but he could name any and every tree on the property, which even now she still found amazing. Most of them were as magnificent as ever, and she enjoyed sitting by them from time to time and resting as she inhaled their sweet fragrance.

Walking about, she noticed a few limbs here and there that had fallen since the last thunderstorm, so she began to pick them up and put them in a pile, which she would burn later or cut and give as kindling to some of the neighboring families who were not as fortunate as she was financially. Alone, there was no one else to really give it to besides them, and it brought her a sense of satisfaction to share what had already been imparted to her. Besides, she could only use so much firewood, and the local forecasts had already predicted an early and cold winter. *Might as well start bulking it up and passing it out.* The task, however, was a bit of an arduous one, as some of the branches were heavier and longer than others. The ones she couldn't pick up, she simply grabbed the end of and dragged along until she had made a large pile near the porch. These, she would cut up and put in bundles for later.

Once she was finished, she walked around some more just as she had done so long ago. It brought back bittersweet memories, but she was glad to have cleaned up the yard a bit and was out of the house for a while. Climbing back up the porch steps, she sat down on the top one and gazed again at the yard before returning to her opulent room and all the things that reminded her of the people she had cared about and lost. She could hear her mother's voice inside her head telling her that she had not "lost" them; they were in heaven where they belonged. But as comforting as that was, it didn't take away the desire to ask God *why* when she felt that she had needed them most. *Try not to keep thinking about them like that,* Lark scolded herself and went to take a long, hot bath. That would be relaxing after all the cleaning, and then she could watch an old but funny movie to reprogram her brain and think of happier things . . . or so she hoped.

The Mission

A miel stood quietly as he waited for his final orders. He had been told he was being sent on a specific assignment and waited silently and patiently for his final debriefing.

"Do you know why I was chosen?" he asked a small seraph that stood directly behind him.

"Are you talking to me?" the seraph replied, looking up at the extremely towering angel and then around at everyone else in case he might have heard wrong.

"Yes," Amiel said. "I was, but from the bewildered look on your countenance, I can detect that you haven't the slightest clue, and so I will not inquire from you again."

"OK," said the timid seraph, clearly perplexed.

Amiel turned back and stood once again in silence, though his mind raced. It had been a while since he had been sent to earth. And it had been short-lived. He had only gone with Gabriel in an effort to deliver a message from God. Being a spectator was more like it; Gabriel had done all the talking. But he didn't mind. He enjoyed it and had learned a lot. It made him feel good to honor the Creator. But when he had heard that he may return to earth for a separate assignment, he stood in amazement. Amiel would make Him proud. After all, he and the other heavenly creatures had been made for one purpose and one purpose only—His glory and will. Earth was so different, so disheartened and full of turmoil. Even the plants and animals were anguished and groaned for the return of the King and for a new earth to begin. One that would exist for eternity and no longer be confined or defined by the constraints of sin and the demonic forces of none other than Lucifer, the fallen one.

Amiel was now very close to the throne and beamed with gratitude. *I guess it really doesn't matter where I'm going, just that I have been chosen,* he reasoned. Letting his wings spread out to their farthest reach, he drew them back as he was called up and announced. Many voices were heard singing, "King of kings, Lord of lords, holy is His name. Who is, who was, and who will be forever." It was a glorious sight and sound to behold.

After he had received his final debriefing, Amiel was dismissed to leave immediately for earth. With the proclamation, he simply had to close his eyes and envision where he was to be sent, and in a blink of an eye, he would be there. While he thought it was an interesting or rather odd assignment, it was never for him to question. He knew that his Creator was perfect in every way as was His will.

Nevertheless, he wondered if this human would be afraid like all the others. Gabriel had told him that each time he had visited a human throughout history, he always had to tell them to not be scared, that their fragile human hearts and disbelieving eyes were their true reason for amazement and fear. Long gone were the days of the first Adam who had walked with God before Lucifer had abandoned the truth and played a deceitful trick upon the other human, Eve. After that, all humans had a sinful nature, and due to its progression like a cancerous disease, were not attune to the spiritual realm. Blinded eyes, darkened hearts. And yet loved above any creation, even angels. He had to admit it was intriguing.

Some of his fellow angels were part of the watchers. They would observe the comings and goings of humans and report. However, those angels were unable to have encounters like the archangels. Unlike the watchers, Amiel could intervene and even fight. He and the other archangels were taller, with a larger wingspan, and given authority including holy weapons to wage war against the evil one and those who would also suffer in eternal damnation at the end of all things. The humans who lived in heaven were no longer in a state of depression, as were their counterparts on earth. They lived and moved about in one accord, in perfect unity, and at perfect peace. The chains of deception had been tossed astray, and all things were made known to them, save one thing: the date and time the King would return for the rest of His people. But even the King did not know this either—only God, the Creator. Continually, they, the humans and the other celestial beings, worshipped. It was the melody of glory, and it always left Amiel with such purpose and perspective.

The world of humans could not grasp such awesome splendor and order, except a chosen few who had lived a lifetime and had been privy to a glimpse without the sting of death. Some had told Amiel that because humans were blinded by sin, they could not see all the magnificence of the Lord; but despite that impediment, some, like he, were called to reveal what the human eye could not see and what the feeble mind could not fathom. It was so touching that such effort was made for mere mortals. It moved him passionately and struck a chord deep within his being.

Smiling, Amiel closed his eyes, and in the twinkling of an eye, he stood in the large yard that Lark called home. Choosing to be patient and take in the tranquility of his earthly destination before immediately greeting her in full grandeur, he walked quietly through the large gathering of trees and paused, gazing on the intricate beauty displayed by the Father. Lark, on the other hand, continued to clean up and make notations to the designs she had drawn as she outlined the changes to each room still left to receive a modern touch, oblivious to the supernatural being now occupying a piece of time and space in her world.

She finished stripping away the last of her dirty and dusty clothes and moved toward the large bathtub. Its bronze claws and old-world style gave it character and a sense of time long past. It had been a rare find for her mother who always enjoyed the eccentric and unique, since most tubs in that era were not made so large and accommodating. Lark recalled the discussion with her father at having found it. He was a more modern and practical purchaser but seemed to melt when her mother would plead with him in earnest for purchases or projects near and dear to her heart.

"Oh, Luke, it's the one. It's perfect."

"Caroline, now wouldn't you prefer one that is a bit more up to date, like with small little jets that can propel the water across your aching muscles, my dear?"

"Not hardly. I wouldn't know what to do with all those new-fangled things they have on the market. This is just fine, honey. It's perfect to me, and I think it will look great in the house. Gonna really be a beautiful piece once I'm done cleaning it up and making it shine like new. So the question is . . . may I have it?" Her eyelashes batted sweetly at her husband.

He had crumbled under her gaze, and she had giggled like a silly child. She never did ask for things that were too extravagant or truly wasteful, but it was amusing to Lark to watch such a strong and stoic man melt into the arms of her mother who he loved so fondly and completely.

It had been a great find, and over the years Lark learned that its value had gone up to the tune of ten times its original asking price. *A find indeed,* she said to herself and turned the faucet water on. She had always enjoyed hot baths, not lukewarm and definitely not cold, but almost scalding. And she was willing to wait until she had the water to her liking. A little mineral salt to sweeten the well-deserved soak, and she knew she could drift away blissfully for a moment to a time when her dreams felt real, before getting out and reminding herself to stay busy to avoid the encroaching depression. The projects propelled her in ways to overcome what in many respects would have debilitated her.

Feeling the warmth of the water, Lark positioned herself comfortably, put a small, rolled white towel behind her head, pulled her long hair into a chignon, and let her head rest back, her eyes closed. Her feet rested on small shards of mineral salts not yet quite dissolved. She played with them childishly to let them accumulate between her dainty toes and then afterward pushed them forward, helping them dissolve further until all had vanished into the water, making it soft and silky. She continued to imbibe upon her favorite activity of each day. Sometimes this ritual would last until her skin had wrinkled on her fingertips, and, other times, if she was beginning to fall asleep, she would go ahead and finish bathing as opposed to simply soaking because she feared drowning in it absent-mindedly. She personally did not know of anyone who had died that way, but her parents had always warned her of such an event, and their warning had stuck. Lark wasn't going to take any chances. Mind you, there wasn't really anyone to call for help.

However, today wasn't one of those days. The walk had revived her, and she did not feel exhausted any longer. The house was as clean as it could be, despite certain materials being stacked in the remaining rooms yet to be repaired and restored. She had drunk her morning coffee, read the local news, and now could sit back and relax with a sense of satisfaction that the day had been extremely productive. In fact, she sensed a weight being lifted off her shoulders, though unexplained. She had noticed a few items in the fridge that needed replacing, so once she was finished, she would probably drive into town and go ahead and do a thorough shopping, so she didn't have to return until next month.

Making a mental list of some of the items, she soaked another ten or fifteen minutes and gingerly stepped out of the tub, towel in hand. It was not uncommon for her to take as many as three baths a day, but for the most part, a morning refresher and afternoon soaker were satisfactory. Lark tried to dry her long hair before it dripped all over the floor, but it was useless. *Oh well.* She grimaced as she finished drying off and putting the towel down on the floor to finish soaking up the puddles of water surrounding her feet, as if holding them hostage. Thankfully, she had not made too much of a mess, and though she knew she would not hold herself to that standard for more than a week or two, she was pleased. Not only for the day and the work that she had done thus far but for the mood she was in. She felt more uplifted, not so sullen and melancholy, and she had no real answer for it. Truly, she felt energized beyond belief. Strangely eager almost for the next event or project that was required or demanded of her. *Couldn't be the coffee,* she mused and laughed aloud. *But . . . what is it?*

She finished dressing and stared once again in the mirror; this time she smiled back. It felt different, but not in a bad way. She picked up the pace, determined now to get to town and get back before the usual influx of people hovered around the main thoroughfare and window shopped for what seemed like hours. Though it didn't bother her as much as it used to, it still brought sweet yet painful memories of what she no longer had. But something felt different as if she wanted to go, wanted to interact, wanted to even—dare to say—smile, unlike all the other instances she might have given a polite nod to but nothing more.

Getting in her old 1950s Ford pickup truck, she turned on the ignition and hummed a song she hadn't heard in years. It was melodious, and as she pulled out from the long driveway, she couldn't help but feel that, somehow, someway, today was going to be very different.

The wind was strong and the road dusty. She whipped around each turn, drawing closer to town, noticing the dust swirling about in the air behind her like a whirling dervish spinning and turning violently to a song not known by humans, but Lark did not want to roll her window up. It was far too pretty a day to not enjoy the sunshine, despite the crisp, cold breeze that passed through her fingertips when she stuck out her hand and forearm along the windowsill of her classic truck. It felt truly exhilarating, and the smile that crept across her face made her heart warm and feel full.

What in the world was happening? Ever since she got out of the tub from soaking, she felt different. She couldn't recall the last time she had been this happy. Was this what she had been seeing as she walked past people smiling and not returning the gesture? *Wait* . . . she thought, suddenly feeling remorse for a second and guilt at the same time. She did recollect a time when she had felt this good, but it was in the presence of her parents. Days when she had basked in their love and felt this same feeling, yet selfishly taking it as something that did not warrant a moment of gratitude. She wondered if this feeling meant she was starting to forget the pain of losing her parents, and she grimaced. She did not want to feel remorse at the newfound stirring within her. "Am I finally letting you both go?" she said aloud toward the sky while she continued driving into town. But it didn't feel as if she was or wasn't. It just simply felt like her entire being had come alive with vitality and vibrancy. Once she got back home, she would be able to analyze it further, but for now . . . just a country road and the beating sun were the only things to ponder.

Not long after, the gravel turned to blacktop, and Lark eased her way onto it as she watched a few speeding cars zoom past her like they were in a race. "Whoa," Lark said, suddenly slamming on her brakes. A truck she had not seen before came speeding forward and would have collided with her had she not stopped. Sweat beads ever so small glistened from her forehead, and she brushed them away as she steadied her heart. "Goodness, that was close," she whispered to herself and again looked intently to her right and left before easing onto the busy thoroughfare.

Glancing in the rearview mirror, she studied her face, ashen and pale from the very recent scare. She tried to relax, the immediate danger gone. She could feel the blood flowing again and her cheeks now turning to their original rosy complexion. Her eyes no longer darting, but calm, focused, and intent on paying attention to each and every movement or situation. All the other intersections had a light, thus dispelling any confusion as to when a person could proceed, but not that one. Most of the time, she would have gunned it, thinking speed would eliminate the need to be so cautious as to who was coming up the road. She was glad she didn't adhere to her normal response. A cautious glance had been a life-and-death decision, and without further ado, she put both hands on the steering wheel and gripped it tight, still riding toward the town despite a little shakiness reverberating through her fingertips.

The main highway was the shortest way into the quaint town littered with small, wooden houses painted in a variety of colors, some sprinkled along the highway and others huddled closely as if every one of them was in one big hug. As she veered closer to town, Lark saw the residences slowly begin to fade and the brightly colored storefronts owned and operated by the townsfolk appear. Most of them also wooden with large handmade signs over the windows, showcasing whatever their specialty or service was. A few were older than most and had fallen into a bit of disarray but not too much of an eyesore. A good weekend's worth of work and a gallon or two of paint would have them looking their best in no time. Perhaps she thought she should offer her services. Probably old couples who could no longer physically repair them and whose kids had moved on to the larger cities. Making a mental note of a few of them that were more declined than others, she vowed to give the owners a call. Besides, it made her feel energized and purpose-filled when she did a little thing or two for the townsfolk without pay, and most of the time without their knowledge, which was always the most rewarding because it was unexpected.

Lark continued to drive farther and farther into the heart of town. There was only one grocery store, a hardware store, and a variety of the boutique shops owned and operated by small families over the years. Most of her schoolmates now ran the businesses their fathers had operated and their grandfathers had helped to start or started back when times were harder but better. Due to her avoidance over the years, she had forgotten a few names along the way, and still there were others whose boisterous and contagious personalities all throughout grade school had blazed imprints in her mind that had remained for years. On rare occasions, she would peer a little into the shop windows, careful to not be observed, with the idea that she might see a childhood friend or two behind a register or perhaps stocking a shelf. But so far, she hadn't really recognized anyone. Lark shrugged, her solidarity suddenly appearing very real to her and the thought that in her grief she had shut out all possibilities of normalcy. Then she pondered if she had really lost out all that much. No busybodies, no extra baggage, and no drama! Her days could be filled with whatever she wanted to do without recourse. All the busyness of people wasn't something she wanted or missed, but to share a little bit of her world with someone, well, that might be nice. *Then again,* Lark mused, *they would try to change things, put their spin on it, and then it wouldn't be my world after all.* Maybe it really was better this way. Shrugging, she parked the truck in the grocery store's parking lot, locked up, and began meandering toward the door.

Daydreaming as usual and not expecting someone to be on the other side, Lark pulled at the front door forcefully and a woman lunged forward, obviously having lost her balance, as she too had reached for the door from the opposite side. Lark almost tumbled over as well when the lady came barreling in her direction.

"Oh, my goodness, I'm so sorry," the lady said, trying to catch herself but managing to bump into Lark anyway. "They've been meaning to put in those newfangled doors that slide open and shut for a while now. Sure wish they would; maybe things like this wouldn't happen." Her face was visibly red and her forehead perspiring from obvious embarrassment. Lark continued to help her gather her items, and the woman continued to ramble and straighten her clothes. "Please forgive me, I've been talking a mile a minute. Are you all right yourself?" she asked, for once pausing between her words and looking into Lark's eyes.

Lark smiled, still somewhat guarded herself. "Yes, ma'am, I am."

The Encounter

H opefully, I did not ruin any of the groceries. Don't need anything leaking out in the car," the woman said, laughing nervously. Lark knew she was simply making polite conversation, so she smiled compassionately back in kind.

"Oh, I agree. Can't stand when that happens," Lark found herself chiming in. Her gregariousness surprised her; in fact, most of her behavior had surprised her since taking her routine bath. However, it didn't make her feel bad, just so unlike her to not be the reclusive little spinster she knew she had become.

The woman smiled at Lark's response, obviously feeling slightly better knowing that things like that happened to everyone and that she wasn't alone in a world of mishaps.

"I'm sorry, I didn't get your name." The woman looked back toward Lark as she headed to her vehicle to put down the groceries suspended in her arms.

"It's Lark . . ."

"Lark?" she said rhetorically.

"Yep, just Lark. Very nice meeting you. Maybe I will see you around . . ." Lark fumbled with the words, not sure if this would be the last time she engaged in random conversation with anyone or not. She knew that while it was now years later, she still had days when the loss of her parents could still hold enough sway to pull her captive in her bed and deep into the covers. It was a day-by-day existence at times when an emotional roller-coaster could dictate everything from sleeping habits to eating ones. So the words of further interaction seemed pointless and difficult to say. The lady, however, did not sense Lark's inner struggle and simply waved while nodding in agreement.

Lark exhaled and turned an about-face to do what she originally came to town for—grocery shopping. Carefully observing this time to not open it at the same moment as anyone else, she drew open the door and quickly walked in and toward the line of empty shopping carts. A hand sanitizer dispenser stood right beside her, and Lark took the time to clean the handle of the cart and her own hands before venturing to the first aisle. She really wasn't a fan of grocery shopping or at least not since she was a kid, and everything back then seemed like a delicious exercise for adults, instead of the painful and nerve-racking chore that she now knew it was. Perhaps if she had companionship like most, it would still be enjoyable, like a small child full of wonder and amazement. Nowadays, these necessary excursions seemed a chore, and it typically aggravated her more than anything. However, today seemed more of a refreshment than a burden.

Lark pushed the cart down the aisle and hummed a small but sweet tune she had not recalled for some time—a melodious one sung by her mother as she sat on the side of Lark's bed to tuck her in on the nights she wasn't working late. The tune of "Love Lifted Me" echoed across her lips, and as other shoppers passed her in the aisle, they smiled and their eyes sparkled to such a delight, much to Lark's dismay and a bit of embarrassment. She had not realized she was humming so loudly. Her face turned bright red, knowing others had heard her.

Continuing to grab items she had on her list, Lark completed the rest of her shopping and moved her cart toward one of the registers. A few had two or three customers already waiting in line, so she tried to peer over them to see if any other lines were shorter or had just opened up. A light flickered from a box that lurched its way upward. It illuminated the number 7, and Lark pushed her cart toward it and to a small, gangly young woman who stood behind it. She was dressed in all black attire, and her fingernails were also painted black. Even her hair was dyed a dark color that did not seem to suit her. Piercings were plenty, and Lark couldn't help but wonder if she was looked at or frowned upon for being different. She wasn't sure if a conversation was appropriate but decided she would step out of her normal comfort zone and extend pleasantries to her as well.

"Hi, how's it going?" Lark asked quickly before her doubt caused her to lose her nerve.

The girl looked up at Lark with very little emotion and then shrugged her shoulders. "All right, I guess," she said sullenly.

"Umm, OK," Lark responded.

The groceries made their way across the conveyor belt one by one, and the beeping of the bar codes left ringing in her ears. She wasn't sure if she should interject something else or just leave the young cashier alone. She didn't seem to want to say much, and nothing was worse than forced communication. Lark bit her tongue as she quietly watched everything finish and kept herself preoccupied by grabbing each of the bags filled with the groceries and putting them nicely back into her cart.

"I saw you help my mom earlier," the girl said, almost mumbling as her head stayed down, looking at the register.

"Oh, really . . . that was your mom outside?" Lark said quizzically.

"Yeah . . . that's her," the girl said, still not making eye contact.

"Well, I didn't mean for her to fall, we just happened to be walking in and out of the front door at the same time. Guess she just lost her balance." Lark eyed her for any type of emotion, but there was none.

"Yeah, she's real clumsy," the girl responded very matter-of-factly.

"Not really, could have happened to the best of us," Lark mused, just trying to be helpful.

"No, she's just clumsy," the girl retorted and rolled her eyes as if in distaste.

Lark cringed. She watched the young woman clearly appear disinterested at the plight of her own mother, and she felt such a pain in her heart. At least that girl had her mother; she had someone to love her back and be around. Lark had no one and couldn't fathom why in the world there was such an aversion and lack of empathy on the cashier's part toward the matriarch and woman who bore her.

"Well, guess it's none of my business, but I think it was just bad timing like I indicated before, and I think she will be just fine in case you were *concerned*," Lark said a bit sarcastically, but only because it bothered her so to see such lack of compassion. The words had little effect. Lark was aghast but said nothing. *So much for my mood of friendliness today,* she mused. Then she felt another twinge of guilt. Is that how she came across to others? Did they perceive her as some uncaring and unfeeling person when they tried to reach out to her, and she herself extended only the cold shoulder?

Lark noticed a lone picture behind the register that was held by a couple of strands of clear tape. It was of a man, woman, boy, and girl. All of them were smiling and hugging one another. She surmised that it was the girl's family and that the lady in the picture was her mother. Lark caught her breath as she recognized the boy in the picture; she shook her head in disbelief. It was the same smiling boy who was in the newspaper that she had just read about before arriving in town. The same picture that had stirred something deep inside of her, but for what reason she did not know. Lark noticed the girl staring at her.

"Ma'am, hello? I said the amount is $227.81."

Lark looked back at the unfriendly cashier as she was jolted back into reality and managed a feeble smile. "Oh, forgive me," Lark said apologetically and rummaged through her pockets for the cash she had brought with her. She wanted to ask the girl about the picture, and her curiosity continued to plead with her to say something as she counted the money and handed it over. But sensibility also begged to be heard, and its voice to not pry or invade privacy won the argument. So she took the change, shoved it into her pocket, and extended a "thank you" after all the bags were securely placed into the cart. She wasn't going to take any chances and have the groceries fall out of her hands as she tried to bring them home. Glancing back at the picture once more, she smiled at the cashier, who did not reciprocate the gesture, and pushed the cart to the front door.

Lark wasn't upset; rather, she was intrigued and determined to find out why the picture had the young boy she had seen earlier in it. Trying to recall what the words had said by the picture of the kid, she let the tailgate down with a thud, finished pushing her groceries to the back of the truck, and then shut the tailgate, making sure it was securely locked in place. She opened the driver's side door, turned on the ignition, and breathed a sigh of relief. She still felt surprisingly good overall but was happy to be back in her dad's old pickup truck and heading back home. There was a small ice cream parlor on the outskirts of town that sounded good, and her rumbling stomach seemed to agree entirely.

Turning the steering wheel to the left after a few miles, Lark beamed with satisfaction at the sight of the quaint ice cream shop at the next intersection. It had been owned by the Barker family, and each one had made his or her own signature dessert. Things such as the waffle cone layered in colored sugar of the Famous Barker "Bonanza" Split. Everything sounded superb, but Lark had only visited the place on good days, ever since the life she had was suddenly cut short and left her heart reeling.

Only a few parking places were left. Around this town, dessert was always on the menu, and the townsfolk continued to flock there daily. Stepping out of the truck after parking it in the farthest slot, Lark exited and straightened her shirt, hair, and jeans. It wasn't so much that she cared necessarily what any of them thought about outward appearance, but looking presentable was, at the very least, an understanding. The truck door slammed with a loud thud, and Lark walked quietly to the door. She could hear revelry and commotion as each conversation became a musical masterpiece full of highs and lows, and every once in a while there was a shrill from out of nowhere as laughter rang out merrily. Lark hesitated. It seemed almost too much . . . too many people . . . too much boisterous noise. She felt as if she might be suffocated in such closed confinements with strangers, and she caught herself as she balanced against a small rail near the door, nausea gripping her stomach like a vice unwilling to let loose.

"Get ahold of yourself," she said quietly but firmly. Slowly, she began to feel the ground beneath her again, and her own heartbeat no longer stampeded the wall of her chest like wild horses.

The nausea disappeared as quickly as it had started, and, regaining her composure, she wiped the small sweat beads from her brow and pulled open the door as if it were a longstanding battle between them. Once inside, the cool air hit her face, and she instantly felt flushed as people stopped in mid-sentence to stare at her.

Oh boy, she thought, and breathed in slowly and deeply. She eyed a small table that sat only two and made her way to it. It was located near a window, unobtrusive and farther back than the rest of the other larger tables. *Precisely what I wanted,* she mused and was grateful that it had not been occupied. Many of the singular guests had sat at the long bar counter, drinking the delicious malted concoctions, and didn't even seem to notice the quiet oasis.

Lark sat down and grabbed the menu. Reading through it was enjoyment itself. Everything sounded wonderful, and the more she read, the hungrier she became. Finally, her eyes spotted an old favorite: a sugary waffle bowl cone with blueberry ice cream and cheesecake bits. The nutritional content was located to the side of it, but Lark purposely put her palm down to cover it. "Not worrying about all that right now," she said, laughing quietly. She tried to wait patiently for the waiter or waitress to take her order.

Moments passed and Lark simply smiled, but as time continued to tick and other people came in and were served, she fought the urge to interject. The patience paid off though as a younger waiter with blue eyes and tousled blonde hair finally approached her.

"I'm so sorry, miss. Been really busy today. What can I get ya?" He rummaged through a small apron pocket and drew out a little notepad and a pen.

"That's OK . . . I thought about eating the menu instead, but figured I should just wait on you," Lark quipped.

"Huh?" the teenager said, clearly not catching on to the joke.

"Never mind," Lark said and went ahead and placed her order.

He continued to smile, putting the paper back into his apron and the pen behind his ear. "Be right back," he said hurriedly and rushed to another table full of people.

Lark shook her head, not really sure if this had been such a great idea after all. *I mean, I do have ice cream in the freezer,* she mused. But she knew it wasn't the same. Something about other people preparing her food always made it taste better, and dessert was no different.

When the absent-minded waiter appeared back at her table, he held a tray with a large crystal dish, and in it sat a beautiful masterpiece of ooey-gooey goodness. Lark grinned ear to ear for the first time in a long time. Like a small child, her eyes danced, and she turned back toward him with the enormous grin still planted across her face.

"This looks really good, thank you."

His tousled hair fell a bit more in his face, and he brushed it away quickly. "Glad ya like it, ma'am. Let me know if there is anything else you need." With that, he laid the ticket already prepared on the edge of the table.

Lark glanced at it for a brief second and then picked up the spoon. Before too long, she sat back with a look of satisfaction. Although there was still plenty of ice cream in the dish, she felt she had made a fairly decent-sized dent in it and now could take a very long nap to finish off the day. Most of the people sitting in the adjacent tables had also finished and, with arms outstretched in an effort to not feel so full, exited the parlor, away to whatever pressing matters needed to be attended to.

Lark grabbed the ticket from the edge and walked toward a cheery lady operating a lone register near the exit doors.

"Everything was good?" the woman asked. She took the ticket from Lark along with the wadded up ten-dollar bill Lark had already taken from her pocket.

"Um, yes, ma'am, very good," Lark whispered sheepishly, thinking about all the unnecessary but delicious calories she had ingested. *Again, try not to think about it,* she scolded herself, but not too convincingly, already thinking of the next time she might venture out to enjoy it again or perhaps something new altogether.

The lady handed a few dollars back, and Lark brought it to the table as a tip before leaving and waving good-bye. She had never been this friendly since she was a kid . . . why now the sudden desire to be so gregarious? Just like the grocery store. Nothing seemed to add up, but she climbed into the truck and headed back home, figuring once she was there everything would return as it was before.

The ride back was far less eventful, and very few cars even passed. The country roads seemed desolate and quiet, thus giving her time to simply be quiet and think. There were still projects that demanded her attention, and though a nap sounded very good, so did the thought of finishing some of the tile work left in one of the walkways and bathrooms. She had purchased a new wet saw to accomplish the task but had not even taken it out of the box, which sat next to the pallet of tile in the foyer. The closer she got to the house, the more her energy increased, as if she had been hooked up to an electrical outlet and now felt the jolts coursing through her—the sensations a bit alarming. Lark bit her lip and shook her head in confusion. *Maybe I really should just go ahead and lie down,* she thought, checking her own forehead for signs of fever. *Nope,* she thought as she put her hand down and back on the steering wheel. No warmth, no fever, no signs of illness. *What is happening to me?* she tried to reason.

Lark traveled a bit farther until she saw the entrance to her home. There in the garden, something sparkled brightly like a crystal that had been illuminated by sunlight at every angle simultaneously, and it was nothing short of blinding. Stopping the truck for a second, she tried to reason in her mind what would be making such a bright light, but nothing in the yard could have been playing such a strange trick to her senses. Lark paused down the driveway, letting the truck idle a bit as she peered out of the window, hoping to get a better look. But still, her eyes could not seem to focus on the large, glowing object. Still shaking her head, she checked in her rearview mirror for anything or anyone else that might be out of place, but everything was as she remembered, except for the unmistakable light. Maybe it was the sun casting shadows against the leaves of the trees, but Lark still wasn't convinced.

She continued to slowly press the gas, steering the old truck to the front of the house. Once there, she parked the truck abruptly and jumped out. She slammed the door behind her, hoping if it was something or someone that they would be afraid by the sudden sound and know she meant business. But no movement ensued. Lark began walking closer, the truck keys in her hand. Step by step she could feel her heart beating quicker and quicker, the thuds bellowing in her ears. Nothing was moving, and the light was getting brighter and brighter. Lark gasped in awe as she tried to catch her breath and drew closer to what she could not explain.

There, radiating directly in front of her and standing over eight feet tall, was a figure of a man illuminated with massive wings that seemed to envelop his entire body—like large hands glowing in brilliance. Lark stood awe-stricken at the massive wings and image of a man clearly not human. Even his hair glowed, and his eyes shone with a sparkle nothing short of ethereal. Lark tried to swallow but couldn't. She knew she was still breathing but struggled with the feeling that she wasn't. However, the sensation itself was not altogether unpleasant. As for her mind and emotions, she seemed completely at peace, and a joy unexplainable permeated throughout her as if nothing else mattered and she was unfettered by the normal trappings of emotion. Only awe, strangely mixed with a sense of fear.

"Do not be afraid," he said, his voice firm, full, and calming.

"I . . . I'm . . . who are you?" Lark managed.

"I am Amiel, a messenger of the Creator, and I have been sent here to offer you something that has never been."

"What? Why . . . why me?" Lark listened to her own voice as she stuttered for the right words.

"The Most Holy One has not told me the answers of which you seek. Therefore, I cannot be responsive at this time. I can only say that He has chosen you, Daughter."

"I have never done anything to warrant Him choosing me for anything. Why would He? I mean, I went to church and stuff like that with my parents a long time ago, and I do believe in Him, but I haven't been going to church for a while. Can't figure out why, of all the people in the world, or whatever 'this' is, He'd pick me. I mean, what I'm trying to say is that I . . ." Lark paused before finishing. "I don't feel worthy of whatever is happening." Lark blinked back the tears from her eyes. The heat and light seemed to warm her skin and make the salty tears sting as they fell down her face. Brushing them away, she smiled feebly.

"That is not for me or you to know at this moment in time, and as I have already indicated, it has not been revealed to me. I do not have much time, so I will discuss with you what I am able and then I shall ask you to make a choice." With that, Amiel drew his hand out and extended it toward Lark.

The Decision

Lark stood trembling, unsure of what she should do. It still felt surreal to her, and despite blinking or batting her eyes, this being was still standing gloriously in front of her. His presence demanded attention, but she was unsure as to whether what he may be proposing was even possible and if it would affect anything else in her life. Would anyone believe her if she told them that she had been visited by an angel? A real one?

She had heard stories, or rather read stories, of other encounters by people regarding angels, but even though they all sounded lofty and beautiful, they hardly seemed plausible. As a young girl, she had also read in the Bible about such things; the problem was, she and many others she knew had dismissed the idea that they still visited people in modern times.

"Will you tell me what this choice is about? Are you able to know what I'm thinking? Like, do angels have telepathy?" Lark asked, deflecting the question he posed.

"You will know the nature of this choice when the Father bestows upon me the right moment to tell you. I cannot know what you are thinking. I can do anything if the Father allows, but at this time I can only detect you are frightened. There is no reason to be." The angel paused. "Please, Lark . . . don't be afraid any longer.

I'm here because you have been chosen, and it is an honor. So rest assured—He has only good and the very best in store for you."

Amiel's voice remained soothing, and Lark felt much more comforted as she weighed his words in her heart and took a deep breath, exhaling slowly. "Do you have to stay here in the yard?"

"No, I can go as I please while I am here, but my time is limited with you."

"Really? I mean, OK, I understand. Do you have to leave once I make my mind up about whatever it is you are here to give me a choice about, or is this something you will be staying with me for?"

Amiel smiled, feeling the timidity of the human he had been sent to. "It's OK, Lark. It's reasonable given the misgivings and lack of clarity for you to feel as if such a thing is inconceivable while at the same time unclear on what it will entail."

Lark nodded her head in agreement as Amiel continued.

"May we walk? I think it will do you some good, and you can show me around as we discuss what I have been given as a message for you. Perhaps, then, you will have a better understanding and can make a decision if you are in acceptance. As you know, the Father only offers and gives free will to His creation. He will never force you, Lark, or anyone else He has ever created or will create. Just like the saving power of our Lord, King Jesus, it is a personal choice. No dictatorship exists when there is only unconditional love."

Lark smiled, feeling a little more relaxed at the angel's proposal, and grasped ahold of his hand. It felt human and yet starkly different. No flaws existed over his entire hand. It shone as did the rest of his body. His grip firm and warm. His smile was contagious, and Lark felt her grin widen and her eyes gleam with newfound excitement.

"Yes, I will walk with you."

Amiel grasped tighter to her hand, turned toward the front of the dwelling, and began walking. His tall stature loomed over Lark's petite frame—almost making her appear like a small child. Looking up at him as they walked, it was as if he were floating. Lark pondered again if she should pinch herself. Did angels talk about stuff like regular people, or should she simply let him do all the talking? She hoped she could ask him about heaven, but that was probably off limits. So she simply bit her lip and continued walking in unison, despite the obvious differences in stride.

"So tell me about how you see the Father."

"God, you mean?" Lark responded.

"Yes, how do you feel about Him? What is your viewpoint?

Lark wasn't expecting that question, though she should have seen it coming. He was of course sent from God. Why did she not think he would ask such a thing?

"Well," Lark said, a bit embarrassed, "I still believe in Him, but it's been years since I went to some form of organized gathering such as church. I don't even read the Bible like I'm supposed to, but ever since my parents died, I think subconsciously I blame Him for what happened. I mean, He is in control, right?"

"Yes, He is, Lark, but in His perfect wisdom, He allows certain events to happen upon the earth to bring people together, hold others accountable, and/or to simply have His children lean on Him—all so that He may be glorified."

"OK," Lark said, "but that still doesn't explain why He would take two good people who loved Him from their only daughter who needed them."

Amiel's eyes looked down at Lark. "Yes, I can sense your anger and resentment, which has evolved from a deep pain within you. But the Father no doubt knew that their purpose, according to His will, had been fulfilled when He took them to dwell with Him forever, which I can attest is far greater than you can even fathom. Would you not wish for the humans you love to be in paradise surrounded by His love and no longer subject to the sin and darkness of the present world?"

Lark frowned, allowing his explanation to sink in. All this time, she had remained aloof to others, reclusive and unable to let her parents' death finally be laid to rest so that she could function a bit better in communicating and interacting with others. Only recently had the feeling come over her in which she felt comfort, encouragement, hope, and dare she admit, joy. Was it the angel's presence? *Is he the one making me feel this way?* Lark thought. Would he stay and continue to make her feel this way? She had not felt such energy and vibrancy before.

Lark and Amiel continued to walk until they stood in front of the porch. "You are coming in, right?" Lark asked, half expecting him to disappear through the exterior of the house and greet her on the inside like an apparition.

"Yes, I will enter your abode with you. But remember what I told you: I don't have much time and must be on my way soon."

"I understand," Lark said perfunctorily, though she really did not. She ushered him to the kitchen area and offered him a glass of water.

"No, thank you," Amiel responded.

"What, you guys don't eat or drink in heaven?"

"We do, just not the type of sustenance you have here," Amiel said.

"OK, well, what do you eat then?" Lark asked jokingly. Her face became somber when she looked back to see the angel bowing his head and clearly not tickled or amused by her playful banter.

"Amiel, I'm sorry," Lark said apologetically. "I really didn't mean to offend you."

"It's quite all right. I will sit down though as we discuss what I was sent for."

"Yes, yes, of course," Lark said and motioned for him to sit down on the couch. She quickly plopped herself down and stared intently at his glowing face with a mixture of fear, again, and anticipation.

"Lark, what I do know is that you have been given an opportunity to go back in time and change the course of someone's life—if and only if you are willing. If you do, you will return once their course has been altered from the path that was originally chosen by them."

"Wow. Why a human? Why wouldn't God just send angelic intervention?" Lark responded, after pausing for a short time, deep in thought.

Amiel smiled. "Because they would have the same interaction you did when you saw me: awe and fear with a mixture of disbelief."

"Yes, but wouldn't that 'shape them up'?" Lark said, using her fingers in quotations as she finished.

"It might," Amiel said, "but it would not be the same. Do not underestimate the power of simple human interaction of one who is willing."

Lark nodded her head, carefully pondering his words. What on earth was she gonna do to change the course of someone's life, and could she go back in time and save her parents from their death?

Amiel sat quietly, and Lark continued to muse over such thoughts without speaking, though her furrowed eyebrows and wrinkled forehead left nothing to the imagination.

"So do I get to go back in time and change the course of anyone I want?"

Amiel put his hands on her shoulders. "Do you mean your parents? I'm afraid not, Lark."

"But why? I don't understand. Why can't I go back and save them . . . warn them . . . bring them back home?" Lark's voice faltered as she tried to stop the tears that fell from her face, stinging her cheeks. "It's not fair," Lark uttered, this time louder and more forcefully, her anger getting the better of her. It's true, she had been bitter toward God, bitter toward the man who was to blame, and bitter toward all those who had not lost their parents. It used to bother her just to see others smiling, seemingly happy and oblivious to other people's pain—her pain.

"And, just why can't I?" This time, Lark stared at him in defiance, more tears still welling up in her eyes.

Choking back even more tears as Amiel turned toward her fully, she felt his wings flutter and a strong gust of wind come across her face as his hand touched hers. The feeling was surreal, something unexplainable, and, despite the feelings of helplessness, a wave of strong comfort and encouragement coursed through her body and jolted her senses. As she tried to steady herself, Amiel held her.

"Is God mad at me? Is that why He is punishing me and not allowing me to see them or save them?"

"No, Lark, quite the contrary. You are deeply loved by the Father, and He would never do something such as that to hurt you. There is nothing He wants more than for His children to draw closer to Him."

"Well, if He isn't going to let me go back to help them, who does He want me to help?"

"You met two individuals today whose souls are in need of help ."

Lark bit her lip as she stepped back in confusion. "I don't understand," she said, fumbling a bit for words. "Who . . . who did I meet?" forgetting in the moment her interactions in town.

"They are in need of healing, though they do not see past the hurt in order to heal."

Lark thought for a moment and scratched her head, trying to recall, and then it occurred to her who she had seen today. Her mind drifted back to the cashier who looked as if she cared for nothing–very lackadaisical, or the sweet but clumsy lady who she had helped after her fall. Did he mean those two ladies? Was there someone else she had looked at or talked to that he might be referring to? Try as she might, she could think of no other. Her forehead creased and her countenance was forlorn, still trying to reason or think before responding.

Amiel could see the visible signs of her struggle and wanted to ease her concern, but he needed to wait a moment for Lark to try to figure it out on her own. Once she realized, she would understand more fully.

Think, Lark . . . think. But all she could think about was those two women—one not paying attention and the other one not caring to.

"Do you mean the cashier and lady at the grocery store? You can't possibly mean them . . . what do I need to go back in time and save them from?" Lark motioned with her hands as she spoke aloud.

"Those are the two women, daughters of God, that I speak of. But there's more, and I do not believe you are searching deep enough within yourself. You can if you choose, or would you like me to help you?"

Lark stepped back defensively, unsure of what he meant. "Help me how? I'm OK . . . ."

"No, you are not, Lark. You still can't see the beauty of the gift given to you and what you can give to others before it is time for you to come home. There's something else today that you did that will connect everything in your mind. Do you wish to stop and try to recall it, or would it be OK if I reminded you?"

"I haven't a clue what you mean, so yes, please explain to me what you say I am missing. The more you tell me, the more confused I am." Lark began to take a defensive stance.

"Do you see the newspaper lying over there?" Amiel motioned to Lark in the direction of the paper.

Lark followed the direction of his hand and walked toward the folded paper. *What now?* she thought. "OK, here," she said, picking it up. "Now what?"

Amiel said nothing, only motioned for Lark to open the paper. Most of the articles were familiar, of course, as she had read it as recently as that morning. *Wait a minute* . . . she mused. She suddenly thought about the picture, the one that gave her pause early during the day. She read the caption: the "smiling, toothy grin." She recognized the cashier as the young girl also in the picture with the handsome young boy.

Lark held the newspaper up in the air as she spoke. "The picture . . . the people I met today are a part of this, aren't they? What happened? Or is this what I can change if I go back in time?"

Amiel nodded his head, knowing that soon Lark would have to make up her mind, and he would have to leave. Would he be given another assignment? Would it be with her? She seemed so fragile and delicate—it was his first time being so close and in such an intimate setting with a human being alone.

"Oh, I see, I've got something to do with this family, right?"

"Yes, if you choose," Amiel responded.

"Did my parents know them or something? I mean, did I have any interaction with them when I was younger, and I need to fix it or something like that?"

"No," Amiel said. "You had no interactions in the past with this family, only that Father wills it that you be given this gift."

"So if I go back in time, who am I actually helping? The women I saw today were very much alive. Somebody turned right when they should have turned left . . . I mean, well . . . I don't mean to be ungrateful or rude, but I still don't get it. Who needs me to change something? The boy in the picture?"

"Yes, Lark," Amiel whispered slowly. "The boy."

"And why is that?" Lark snapped and instantly felt remorse at having spouted sarcasm to a heavenly being. Feeling the need to be a tad more humbled, she put her head down a bit, waiting patiently for his response.

Amiel watched Lark and breathed in fully.

Lark piped up, uncomfortable with the silence. "I didn't mean to be ugly. I'm very sorry. I just miss my parents so much that trying to look past that has been difficult for me. The truth is, I haven't ever gotten over their death, and I don't see ever getting past that. Even on the days that seem a little better, all it takes is one simple thing to make me crumble and stay underneath the covers, sometimes for days. I figured it would go away, but it hasn't. And you think I'm just gonna go back in time and help somebody else when I can't even seem to fix myself? I hardly think I'm qualified. Why do you keep asking this of me? If I tell you no, will you just disappear?"

"Lark, I didn't ask you; *God chose you*. Why is it so hard for you to recognize that He has a purpose for you also? Yes, I will be departing, but either your life goes back to the way it was—broken as you yourself have attested to and missing purpose—or you choose to live beyond your own pain and suffering in order to meet the needs of another."

"But I don't even know the guy," Lark said emphatically.

"Lark, are you saying what I think you are? That you can only be kind or are willing to help those you know and love? Are you not *all* the Father's creation? Are you unwilling to bestow kindness without condition?"

Lark shook her head, feeling a bit guilty. She knew he was right and that she had been taught otherwise by her parents. They had always taught her to look for the good in others and to be good to all whether known or unknown. Stranger or kin.

"OK, you have made some valid points. I'll do it," Lark said aloud, mulling Amiel's words in her head.

"Good, I was hoping that I could give a report back that your spirit was in agreement."

Lark smiled feebly, wondering what she was getting herself into. She held her tongue and waited somewhat anxiously at what would now take place with her recent decision. Would she just vanish into thin air? Would he?

Lark blinked her eyes, half expecting to be whisked away like something she had seen in a movie. But after squinting a bit, the angel stood regally and without movement in front of her, silent, stoic, magnificent.

"Well," she said, a bit disappointed there were no theatrics, "thought something was gonna happen, but I'm still here and so are you. So what gives?"

"Be patient, Lark. You and I go when the Father is ready."

"Do you think it will be today? Do I need to do anything before I go or something?"

"No, just be patient and do not fear."

"I'm not afraid! OK, maybe a little," she retorted with a small *humph*.

"Time in heaven is not like how it is for those who live on earth," Amiel said.

"Well, I—" Suddenly, Lark stopped mid-sentence. She felt her body tingle and saw a light come over Amiel that seemed to illuminate him even more so than he already was. Lark could not speak. The light was getting too bright, and though she squinted, she could no longer detect the form of the angel that had just been standing before her mere minutes ago.

The tingling subsided, but her eyes still refused to readjust. *Just close them,* she thought, but curiosity would not let her. She continued to peer out, searching for anything detectable that she could lock her gaze and focus on. But for what she did not know, it was near to impossible.

Finally, as Lark was about to give in and shut her eyes, a small figure appeared to move closer and closer to her. Alarmed, Lark brought her hands up as if to shield the would-be intruder.

"Step back," she heard herself say loud enough to bridge the distance.

But the figure continued to draw closer.

"I said step back. I'm not playing. I don't know you."

The figure continued to draw closer but not as fast.

Why is this happening? Lark thought, now feeling frightened. She knew they could hear, so if they weren't stopping, then there must be intended harm. Her voice failed her, but her hands remained extended toward the shadowy figure. *Help!* she thought, but try as she might, nothing came out of her mouth in the form of audible speech. *Is this what is intended by my heavenly visitor?* Lark's mind and heart continued to race. She could feel cold, damp earth underneath her, and her hands and face were cold. It felt like winter, but how was that possible? Was she still on her property?

She wanted to let out a scream, and her eyes continued to have a distorted vision as the shadowy visitor proceeded to dance closer and closer. Lark put her hands over her face and screamed at the top of her lungs, this time forcing it out of her being and hearing it in her own ears audibly.

The First Soul

"Why, honey . . . I'm not here to hurt ya," a small female voice uttered, still chuckling.

"Huh?" Lark replied. She was rather surprised to know it was an older female standing before her and was visibly embarrassed that she had screamed aloud like a frightened child.

The elderly woman tried to extend her hand, but Lark refused as politely as she could, still embarrassed by her lack of composure earlier.

"I've got it. I mean, I'm quite all right," Lark announced, pulling herself up from a bed of frozen earth and dried, decayed leaves.

Once up, she brushed off any remaining dirt and studied the layers of clothes she was wearing. The crispness of the air and pungent aroma of fallen leaves solidified in her mind that it was almost winter, and somehow, someway, she was already dressed for it in clothes she did not recognize but was instantly grateful for.

"I couldn't just leave you out here in the cold," the rather simple and straightforward woman began again.

"Leave me out?" Lark quizzed.

"Why, yes. Lord only knows what in the world you were doing out here all by yourself. You should know better than that. You were climbing trees or something? I mean, did you fall? What in the world would have persuaded you to climb up there?"

"Whoa, lady—" Lark chimed in, wiping a few strands of hair away from her face. "Easy on the questions. How 'bout I ask you a few. Like where am I?"

"Aha!" she shrieked. "I knew it; you don't even know where you are. I'm calling for the doctor."

"No, no . . . there is no need of that. I'm gonna be just fine," Lark said, starting to feel a bit worried if questioned. "Perhaps a good hot chocolate and getting out of this cold will do me a world of good," Lark interjected as she pat the woman on the shoulder.

The sharp eyes of the old female looked at her suspiciously, but she shrugged her shoulders and nodded in agreement to Lark's reasonable proposal.

The arduous trudge in silence left Lark still puzzled about how to address her bearings with such a crotchety old woman, hoping to not raise any further eyebrows. Where would she sleep? Who was going to take her in? Did she even have any money? Thoughts swirled in her head as she tried to think what the best course of action was. The more she thought, the more the voices of doubt tried to creep in, and she felt herself becoming anxious with a knot in the pit of her stomach.

Her newfound guide did not seem perturbed in the slightest, despite her labored breathing and heavy footsteps. Lark felt worried, but she was too nervous to ask her. Just as she had gotten the courage to ask, a small log cabin appeared on the horizon, and a small light illuminated a wooden porch. Lark realized it wasn't far to go before she would have to look—and look fast—in the house to find something that said where she was and when. Glancing around with so few landmarks and indicators made it difficult to narrow down what town and what year she was in. The angel was sadly no longer in sight for her to inquire any further.

The little lady was the first to climb up the steps and stomp her feet. The dirt, falling off into clumps, seemed to irritate her. She finished, using the back of her heel to brush it off the wooden porch with disgust.

"Well," she said, looking a little bit more perturbed than before, "you got a name?"

"Lark."

"Lark? What kinda name is that? Ain't that a bird?"

"Umm . . . yes, ma'am. It sure is. My parents picked it. I had no choice in the matter. But I'm used to it now and am fond of it."

The frail woman looked her over as if mulling over her words and nodded her head again. "Yep, I figured you for one of them city folks from Plantersville. People around here don't have them kinda names." Her country accent thick as she spoke.

Plantersville? Does she mean "Plantsville"? Lark thought as she tried to log every tidbit of information that she could learn about her whereabouts.

"But you sure ain't dressed like one of them highfalutin kind. You dress like one of us." She seemed puzzled, the mixture of what she seemed comfortable with and what she could not comprehend. But before she could speak, her mind seemed to stop her, and, shrugging her shoulders again, she opened the door and held it as Lark went in and she followed immediately after.

At first, Lark seemed amazed at the vast display of trinkets, but the smell of something warm and delicious permeated the room. She lost focus, as she could feel her stomach making those rumbling noises she so dreaded. "Ugh," she mumbled. Grabbing her stomach to stifle the sounds, she walked through the rest of the living room, looking about.

"Well, being as we are now somewhat acquainted, I might as well introduce myself. I am Alva."

Lark turned around as the old woman spoke, only to find a hand extended out directly in front of her, demanding an audience of some sort. Lark tried not to giggle at the silliness and shook Alva's hand profusely, as if formalities were necessary.

"Nice to meet you, Alva!" Lark exclaimed, pumping her hand up and down.

Alva looked as if her guest had lost her mind, so Lark quickly stopped and rubbed her sweaty hand along the side of her bulky clothes. Now that they were inside the cabin, the heat had intensified, and Lark found she wanted to lessen the heavy, suffocating layered fabric before she turned into a giant sweat drop.

"Ms. Alva, do you mind if I take my jacket off? I'm getting rather warm."

"Well, course you can. Was waiting for you to ask me. You look like an Eskimo, but I can't say too much 'cause I'm used to this biting cold and don't wear as much as I used to."

"So is there a mister?" Lark asked, looking about, not wishing to surprise anyone.

"No, he's been gone for decades. Just me now, though my grandkids will be coming to visit soon." Her wrinkled face beamed with pride.

"Oh, really?" Lark responded. "And where are they from?"

"From the city, like it appears you are. In fact, you might know them. My daughter married a man with the last name Williams. Darnell is his name," she shrugged. "He and I don't always see eye to eye. Between you and me, he should be treating my daughter better, but—" she shrugged as she finished, "—she won't listen."

Lark paused, wanting to know more but afraid that if she spoke, it might cause Alva to bottle up and say nothing further. She could tell with such little company Alva wanted to desperately speak her mind, and Lark had nothing better to do but listen. In fact, the more she could glean, the more she could figure out how she was supposed to help.

"So tell me more about your daughter. Why won't she listen?"

"Well, for starters, she is blind as a bat as to her husband's selfishness and lack of participation in his children's lives. My grandkids are growing up, and if he doesn't get his head out of the sand, *he* is gonna miss it."

"Wow, he sounds like a real piece of work! How old are your grandkids?"

Alva paused. "Well, my granddaughter is fifteen, and my grandson is twelve. Like I said, almost grown. My granddaughter is a bit on the dark side . . . eyes painted like a crow. Don't know what she thinks about all day because she hardly speaks to me like she used to. Her mom says it's a phase, but I just don't see it. I think there is something more, and I wish my daughter would see, but she just doesn't seem to hear anything I tell her. No matter how much I plead with her, she just laughs and brushes things off like nothing is wrong and that all things are just gonna come together all by themselves. As if!" Alva folded her hands on her lap and let out a long, exhausting sigh.

Lark wanted to do more, say more, but now wasn't the time. There was something more she needed to know and, if her instincts were correct, then she needed Alva to continue.

"So your daughter is married to someone who doesn't appreciate her, and your granddaughter is into 'goth,' but you haven't mentioned one thing yet about your grandson. Tell me about him. You did say they were all coming to see you soon, right? Might as well get a heads up so that I can greet them properly."

"Well, I was getting to him. He is my pride and joy. He is talented academically and athletically. Handsome and tenderhearted, completely unlike my son-in-law. It's like he was adopted or something. Doesn't make any sense how his older sister just sits and does nothing except dye her hair darker, and he is helping out the neighbor's kid with tutoring, scoring touchdowns on the field, or helping me repair things around this old place. Fact is, I wish he could just get dropped off tomorrow and everyone else skedaddle."

"Oh, you don't mean that, do you?"

"Well," Alva paused. "I mean, a part of me does, though I do love my daughter and both of my grandchildren. I just get frustrated sometimes with all the unnecessary drama from time to time. It gets to be too much for me, and as my years keep getting higher and higher in the digits and my time shorter and shorter, I just find myself becoming less patient for all of that. I want the focus to be on enjoying ourselves, working on projects, and fellowship. The only one who seems to get that is my grandson." Her face beamed as she called his name. "Joseph. He is my little charmer. I can't wait to see him."

Lark laughed, admiring the tenacity of this older woman. She liked Alva already, even if she was a bit unorthodox and unrefined. Lark wondered how long the lady would let her stay. She knew the questions that would soon be thrown in her direction, and she had to formulate responses in her mind so her answers did not sound forced.

"Dear God, help me know what to do," she whispered quietly, the thought of praying foreign to her from years without practice.

"Well, I'm assuming while you are here we can call your family, right? Let them know you are OK." Alva eyed her visitor as she spoke, attempting to read what her guest had not already voluntarily offered.

"Well, Ms. Alva, I live alone. So there is really no one to call. I'm older than I look. So if you don't mind me just staying the night, I'll be on my way before you even realize. In fact, I won't even bother you on the way out."

"Humph . . . you leave just like that, huh? Well, be my guest, but you are more than welcome, my dear, to join us tomorrow. I'm cooking a roast, and if you aren't too busy climbing trees, you can stay over for a good hot meal—ha!" Alva said, chuckling, proud of her quick retort.

Lark laughed too, though she knew better, wondering how much time she would have. "Well, I definitely appreciate the warm abode, and roast is one of my favorites," Lark said, smiling. She moved toward the small couch where a warm blanket sat, welcoming a warm hug to her small body.

"Tired?"

"Yes, ma'am, very," Lark responded, letting out a long yawn.

"All right then, enough of my rambling. I'm headed to bed myself," Alva snorted, breathing deeply as she stood up and rubbed her knees as if arthritis or some other ailment had taken its toll on her.

"Are you OK, Ms. Alva?"

"I'm fine. The weather isn't a friend to achy joints or aging bones. No need to worry; it is simply a by-product of age and a life *actually* lived. I bet no city slicker could hang. They would not have been able to quit twiddling their fingers and they would be unable to figure out how to make a decent cup of coffee without pressing a button. Oh wait, that's where you're from, huh?"

"Well . . ." Lark said, about to defend herself.

"Oh, hush, doesn't matter," Alva said quickly and patted her on the shoulder. "You seem pretty cool in my book, and I'm keeping you from getting some good shut-eye. So with that, consider this good night."

"Good night, then, Ms. Alva. Thank you."

"Welcome," Alva muttered a bit under her breath. She walked slowly down a narrow-carpeted hallway, which Lark could only assume led to her bedroom. The living room was now very quiet. Lark positioned herself down on the couch and pulled the blanket over her. Once Alva was asleep, Lark planned on looking around a bit to see if she could deduce a few things before others showed up and she wouldn't have the time or privacy to do so. The blanket smelled old and mildewed, but Lark put it around her anyway and cradled her head with her hands. Mere moments ago, she stood in her own house, and now, upon divine agreement, she was lying down in a strange place in the home of a woman she barely knew, all because she believed she could make a difference.

Not wanting to fall asleep, Lark tried her best to listen for any sounds from the elderly woman. But all was quiet, and the silence did little to help the situation. Before long, Lark could not keep her eyes open and had drifted to sleep, dreaming of her parents and pretending they were still alive to hold her hand.

***

"WAKE UP!"

Lark's eyes fluttered for a bit as she tried to surmise whether or not she was still dreaming. "Huh?" she replied, trying to rub her eyes and look around.

"Wake up. I've made some coffee . . . not sure if you want some. But if ya do, you can help me in the kitchen and make yourself a cup. There's nothing fancy, just regular."

Alva walked into the kitchen with Lark shuffling sleepily behind her.

"Do you drink that?" Alva asked, pouring her own cup and squinting her eyes at Lark.

"Sometimes. I don't drink it as often as I used to, but I still enjoy it a lot, and I will definitely take you up on the offer."

"Good. We got a lot to do if you plan on sticking around. Since it's gonna be another long and cold evening, we need to have a good warm meal ready and plenty of firewood on the porch so we can keep that old wood-burning stove going through the night."

Lark was so upset that she hadn't woke up to prepare herself a little better, but she would have to *wing it*, and it seemed Alva wasn't too eager for her to leave. Noticing that Alva had stepped further into the small kitchen to refill her cup, Lark eyed a shadowbox on the wall, which held a newspaper clipping and picture of what appeared to be the largest pumpkin she had ever seen, with a beaming Alva holding up a shiny blue ribbon. The caption read, "Local grower wins 1st place." The city on the newspaper read, "Evangeline Herald," and the year, "1972." *Huh?* Lark thought, a bit perturbed. That was her town, the same one she had gotten groceries in just a day before, only this was ten years ago. What in the world was going on? Was this some sort of joke? Had she dreamt all of this up, including the angel? "No, can't be," she said, pinching herself hard and blinking rapidly. It was real . . . just not like what she had imagined. What was she still doing in her own neck of the woods? What had happened ten years ago that had to be fixed, and how did it relate to that ornery but good-hearted woman?

Lark was still thinking to herself when a loud thud caused her to turn and awaken her from her confusing thoughts.

"Here," Alva said, pushing a steaming cup of coffee toward Lark's hands. "You seem lost in la-la land. I figured I'd go ahead and pour yours. Don't get used to it though . . . you aren't paralyzed . . . *humph.*"

Lark tried to keep from laughing. Try as she might to make one think otherwise, Alva had a heart of gold, and it took all Lark had not to burst in a fit of laughter and tell her to lighten up. It was perfectly OK to bare her heart occasionally, right? As Lark pondered her own reasoning, a twinge of guilt loomed in her conscience, and, feeling she had built up so many walls, the idea of taking them down seemed like too much of an undertaking. "Breathe," Lark mumbled to herself as she turned toward the couch, holding her coffee and making sure to walk slowly to avoid even a single drop falling onto the floor. Once she was situated on the couch, she positioned the blanket far enough away and sat down on one side, an armrest helping to give her a makeshift table.

"Thank you, Ms. Alva, for the coffee," Lark murmured, taking a sip and realizing instantly it was still a bit too hot.

"Not a problem. This way, you can sit for a moment and tell me more about yourself."

"Oh, you don't want to be bothered with that, Ms. Alva. I'm rather boring," Lark muttered.

"Boring, you say?" Alva sat almost choking on her coffee as she laughed. "You do know I found you, having falling from a tree and all by yourself. Can't be that boring!"

The fragrance of the coffee was rich with a pungent smell, making Lark feel at ease. She couldn't recall a time that she had sat down and enjoyed it as much with anyone. But revelations like these made her sad and, once again, echoed a life completely and utterly shut out from the outside world. The same things that so many took for granted, she now cherished, feeling that maybe there was hope for her now. She had a mission, a purpose, even if she didn't understand what all was happening.

The coffee went down smoothly, and Lark continued to sip it ever so slowly, trying to play coy with Alva, though it wasn't working too well.

"So what I'm gathering is you just plan on staying a bag of secrets, huh? Well, suit yourself, but if you go on being that way, let me just lay down a few ground rules before you head back to wherever it is you come from. I won't stomach a liar, cheater, or thief. I don't really have much, but what I do have you will respect," Alva said stoically, though she looked rather ridiculous saying it with her hair in disarray, a tattered robe tied around her, and oversized slippers that needed a good washing.

Lark looked at her and managed a smile. "I have no intention of doing any of those things, Ms. Alva. I will be leaving this afternoon to head back home, and while I am here I intend to only be a blessing and a help. Tell me, how long have you lived here?"

"Oh, so you don't wanna answer my questions, but you want me to answer yours? Now that's interesting."

Lark blushed.

"It's all right," Alva said. "Lucky for you, I like talking, and you seem like good company. So I'll answer your question. It's been over forty years. Never really had a desire to go anywhere else, and why should I? It's perfect here. I've got all the land I need to grow my vegetables and plenty of room to avoid the neighbors. Ever since my husband died, I just sit back and enjoy a peaceful sunset or maybe a coffee when the sun is just about to shine across my porch and welcome me to say, *You are still here, you are still alive,* and *you are not alone.* That's what I enjoy. That's where I find my peace . . . my 'me' time. Without worrying about everything like my daughter does. Speaking of, let's finish up the coffee and get to making that meal for them, or we will wind up not finishing by the time they arrive."

"Good, sounds like a plan, Ms. Alva," Lark said, gulping the hot coffee that burned its way down.

Alva watched Lark wince and try to hold in her emotions— but Alva said nothing. Alva motioned for Lark to follow her to the kitchen where she took both cups and set them down on the counter. "So any experience in the kitchen?" Alva asked, turning up her nose. "Whether you do or don't, it's time to get busy."

The First Soul
(Continued)

"Yes, ma'am, I do. I'm not that young. What all do you want to make?" Lark responded as she rolled up her sleeves.

"Well, I had in mind to cook that large roast right there, cut up some potatoes and carrots and onions, and then a few more sides would do nicely. Think you can manage that?" Alva said laughingly.

"Why, I think I can manage to hold my own," Lark said, smiling back at her.

"OK, good, let's get started." With that, Alva put on her apron and bent down near a cabinet filled with a variety of mismatched pots and pans.

"Need any help with that?" Lark asked, trying to be polite.

"No," Alva said very matter-of-factly, "but you can begin peeling the potatoes and carrots. We'll need to put all the vegetables and meat in the slow cooker at the same time so they can cook nice and tender. I'm gonna prepare the meat though because I'm pretty particular about how I brown it and cook it. I'm afraid if you prepare the roast it won't end up the way I do it, and they won't like it. My grandkids absolutely love my roast and potatoes, so when you finish peeling, just turn your head in this direction and simply watch me."

Lark nodded as she grabbed the sack of potatoes and began opening it up while glancing around for a sharp knife. Alva also worked quickly as she seasoned the meat, and soon the sizzle of browning meat echoed into the small kitchen, giving a strong and sweet smell as it cooked.

Before too long, Lark was finished with the potatoes and carrots, so she set the knife on the counter, cleaned up the peelings, and looked behind her where the stove was, not really prepared to see Alva staring at her.

"Something the matter?" Lark asked, feeling a bit defensive.

"No, just wondering what you were humming over there while you were peeling. Sounded familiar, but I can't seem to recall it." Alva continued to rotate the roast in the pan, trying to get each outside edge the perfect shade of golden brown. For a moment, she placed the spatula on the counter and reached for the coffee grounds from the canister to make a fresh pot for later.

"Oh, I didn't realize I was humming it loud enough for you to hear. It's an old hymn my father sang to me. It's called, 'Great Is Thy Faithfulness.' Do you know it?"

"Bits and pieces. I knew it sounded familiar, but it's been ages since I've been to church."

Me too, Lark thought, feeling regret. Ever since she had seen God's messenger, she had felt more and more grievous that she had not made it a point to continue after her parents died.

"Does he not sing it to you anymore?" Alva asked as she picked up the spatula to rotate the sizzling roast once again.

Lark bit her lip. "He's already in heaven, Ms. Alva, so he doesn't sing it to me, but I'm sure he is singing." Lark tried to sound upbeat as she spoke the words, but inwardly she felt a deep sadness.

"I'm sorry to hear that, my dear. Best not talk about it and bring back the tears. Here, come watch me now and learn a thing or two." She put her hands on her hips as if she meant business and took a sip of her remaining coffee.

What a funny little woman, Lark thought, *but I like her.*

Lark finished wiping off the counter, grabbed her cup of coffee, and stood near the stove, far enough away so as to not be in the way but close enough to see. Pressing herself against the countertop, she lifted up her head and peered into the pot where the meat was still sizzling.

"How long does that take?" Lark asked.

"I'm about finished with the browning. Once I'm done with this portion of preparation, I'm gonna stick it in a slow cooker and let it cook through to the point when it's nice and tender." Alva turned the stove off and grabbed the slow cooker from the bottom cupboard. "Let me show you how to put all the food together in here," she said as she plugged in the slow cooker. She carefully transferred the browned roast into the cooker and added a variety of seasonings to cover the meat. "Go ahead and pour all the vegetables in here around the meat," Alva instructed Lark. "We will cook it all together on low for 6-8 hours, so it'll be done just in time for our guests' arrival."

Lark did as she was told, making a mental note of each step and every ingredient used. Once she returned home, she hoped she would have a recollection of her journey and be able to make this meal herself when she thought about such an interesting and amusing woman.

"Later, we can make something for dessert. No meal is complete without that," Alva snorted indignantly.

"Oh, I do like dessert! I have a passion for sweet things," Lark said, trying not to lick her lips as her stomach began to make gurgling noises. To keep busy, she washed the utensils they had just used.

"From the looks of it, you sound hungry for some already," Alva said, pointing to Lark's stomach and giving her a playful jab.

Lark jumped suddenly.

"Did I hurt ya or something?" Alva asked, wondering why her guest had been so alarmed at such a playful and silly gesture.

"I'm fine . . . you just scared me, that's all," Lark said, knowing full well this was not entirely true. She just hadn't been touched, hugged, or anything since her parents died. The touch of another human had felt foreign to her, causing her to recoil. She knew she had upset Alva by her reaction but couldn't explain who she really was. As it was, Alva didn't appear to be buying the whole "scared" story.

Lark could feel the atmosphere inside the kitchen change; a little more reservation and aloofness lingered in the air. She wanted to say something more about it, but what? What could she say or, more importantly, *should* she say to ease the tension without it raising a flurry of questions to which she did not ever want to discuss?

Alva didn't speak for a few awkward moments "Well, that oughta do it for now," she said, setting the glass lid on it, sealing it down until further inspection.

Lark smiled warmly back at her, hoping this could be conveyed to Alva and diffuse some of the building tension that still lingered. "Mind if I make myself another cup of coffee, Ms. Alva?"

"Yep . . . but on one condition."

"What is that?" Lark said quizzically, still unsure if Alva was upset.

"You make me one too!" Alva chided.

Lark grinned. "Sure thing. I'll make them right now," Lark said, exhaling a grateful sigh.

"Good, I have a lot to do today before my daughter arrives. I need to get dressed and start straightening up around here. The firewood I cut last month isn't really dried out, but it should burn, and we can have a nice bonfire after we eat since it's so cold outside. I might even have some hot cocoa left from the last bonfire."

"Really?" Lark replied, excited. "I'm actually looking forward to doing that, and I'm very good at starting fires. My father used to make ones with me when he'd clear off the property, and I'd sit with him for hours just staring at it, barely saying a word. Don't think I've done that in years." Lark caught herself and quickly quieted her voice. The truth was, she hadn't lit a fire without him. But boy how she missed such quiet and happy moments when she felt like she was his princess, like she understood him better than anyone.

Alva looked at her and frowned. "So why'd ya stop? You were going a mile a minute. What's changed?"

"Oh, nothing. Just realized we got a lot to do, and I was feeling like a blabbermouth."

Alva continued to purse her lips together, clearly not convinced. However, much to her credit, she didn't skip a beat, and, sitting in her chair, she cleared her throat. "Well, how about that coffee then?"

"Yep, I'm on it," Lark said. She took a deep breath and walked back into the kitchen where she had set both mugs down on the counter and gently lifted the carafe, still half full, of steaming robust coffee. "Mmm," she mumbled to herself. "One spoonful of sugar or two?"

Lark echoed her question as Alva, sensing her confusion, yelled out, "Two and a half. Ha! Bet you didn't think of that one. I like mine extra sweet."

Both ladies laughed as Lark brought the second helping of caffeine to her.

"Yep, you're all right, Lark . . . you're all right."

Lark sat back down with her in the living room and made herself comfortable before putting the mug to her lips and taking a sip. She knew better this time and blew ever so slightly across the rim of it in an effort to cool it down.

"Best be careful. I burnt my tongue earlier," Alva said very matter-of-factly.

"Really?" Lark said. "Me too. Trying to be more cautious this time, I assure you."

"Thatta girl," Alva said, slapping her knee with a *humph*. "Think I'm gonna take the same advice."

Lark continued to look around the room as Alva fumbled for a remote that appeared to have wedged itself into the crevices of her chair. She still hadn't gotten dressed for the day, but the television seemed to become a priority.

"Need some assistance?" Lark asked, watching her newfound friend searching frantically for the device.

"No, I'm just fine. I just noticed the time! They were supposed to air something on the news about my grandson's team this morning. They won the state championship, and I wanted to catch it and see if they are doing a full segment and if they might have interviewed him or something. He's the pitcher for the team, so they might have." She seemed lost in another world as she fumbled, poked, and prodded at the chair's cushion.

Lark knew better than to go help her, as it would only be taken the wrong way. So she quietly sipped her coffee and continued to watch Alva become further and further incensed.

"What about thinking where you saw it last?" Lark asked.

Alva didn't say a word, seemingly more and more perplexed. "I'm gonna miss the darn show," she said, mumbling angrily to herself.

"I'm sure the TV itself has a power button that we can press for the time being, and then once we find the remote, we can put it on whatever channel it's supposed to be on. And if you don't find the remote, pretty sure the TV's got buttons on it for the channels as well."

Alva looked up briefly and nodded. "Yes, you are right . . . good idea. Just frustrates me that I can't find the stupid contraption. I can't stand to lose things; it's a slap to my memory. You know what I mean?"

Lark laughed. "Ms. Alva, I forget stuff the same as you, and it's not just because of age, or at least not necessarily. When I get busy or when I get overwhelmed, I unintentionally misplace or forget things as well. And just like you, I get frustrated. It happens."

Lark walked over to the TV in search of a power button. "Look, here's the button right here," Lark continued, pointing down to a small, black button labeled "Power" on the right side of Ms. Alva's television set.

"OK, press it. If it is playing, we won't have missed much!" Alva exclaimed, her hands wringing in the air and small wisps of hair falling out of the tightly wound bun that crowned her head.

Lark nodded and extended her right hand until her fingers touched the button squarely, and the TV soon came to life with the volume up fairly loud. Lark stepped back, reeling from the noise, not expecting the blaring sound.

"Wow, that's entirely too loud," Lark said, now reaching for the volume button.

"Don't touch that," Alva snapped.

"Touch what?" Lark retorted.

"The volume button. I have it just where I like it and can hear it clearly. If you mess with it now, it won't be right, and I'll never get it the way it was."

"Ms. Alva, it tells you what number it's on so that if you adjust it, you can readjust it later."

Alva looked at Lark but didn't say a word. Lark couldn't help but feel that once again she had offended the old woman by making her feel less intelligent, though she was only trying to be helpful.

The silence between the women was soon broken by peals of laughter as Alva, who had continued to search for the remote, now lifted her hand with her prize. "I knew it was here!"

Lark exhaled, again deeply happy that her generous beneficiary had not been offended, or if she had been initially, she no longer was. "Awesome! Now I can finish my coffee and watch that really talented grandson of yours," she said, now sitting back on the couch and picking back up the coffee mug that sat on a small round table next to the couch.

The sound from the TV was still very loud, too loud, but Lark was getting used to it and could stomach the noise if it mattered that much to Alva. A few clicks of the remote and Alva found what she was looking for: the KLFY channel. She set the remote on the end table next to her own chair.

Lark wanted to laugh aloud as she observed Alva eyeing it before setting it on the table. An obvious result of having lost it moments earlier in her seat cushion.

Not realizing Lark was watching, Alva picked up her coffee and began drinking it as she eased back in her chair. The news anchors were talking amongst themselves, and a picture of a junior high team popped up behind them with the caption: "Local Team Wins! State Champions Headed to Nationals."

"This it is, there it is!" Ms. Alva exclaimed, and Lark almost choked.

There on the screen was the familiar, toothy grin of the boy in the newspaper! Had she not swallowed most of her coffee beforehand, she would have spewed it out in surprise and confusion. "THAT'S YOUR GRANDSON?" Lark finally managed to blurt out, pointing exactly to the one she believed him to be.

"Yes, that's him. Handsome, huh? But how did you . . . ." Alva seemed a bit perplexed but did her best to keep her eyes focused on the television set as more pictures flashed on the screen with the video of the actual game.

Lark didn't say another word, still trying to make sense of everything. *What in the world?* she thought, now sitting on the edge of her seat. Her coffee was finished but the empty mug stayed put, clearly of no great importance anymore.

The sports segment ended shortly thereafter, and Ms. Alva got up to check on the food that had been cooking for a while now in the kitchen. Lark immediately jumped up as well to assist her, but Alva motioned for her to simply sit and watch the news in case there were any more stories about her grandson.

Lark nodded in agreement.

Alva took one look into Lark's cup and took it from her hands before walking out of the room.

"Thank you," Lark said a little too loudly. But Alva was already in the kitchen, and if she heard, she never did say.

Lark looked back at the television screen. This was the kid who needed saving. But from what? Looked like he had it all together. Was something going to happen today when they came over? Was she gonna have to rescue him from a speeding car (not that there were any) or maybe perform the Heimlich maneuver? Whatever it was, she needed to find out more if she could before they showed up.

Alva had finished checking the food and now walked down the hallway again toward what appeared to be a bedroom with a bathroom directly adjacent to it.

Lark mused, realizing she didn't have any other clothes to change into, and it just didn't feel right breaking her usual bathing regimen. She hoped that Ms. Alva would have something she could wear so she could at least get a shower or bath and feel clean, but the prospect of that was slim, though Ms. Alva was of a petite stature herself.

She also wondered if when she intervened, or whatever you called it, would she be taken away just like how she had appeared, with no time to say good-bye? Or what if she couldn't save him, did she still vanish in a blink of an eye or get to repeat it? When would the angel appear again, or would he?

Lark's mind continued to race at a breakneck pace, so much so that she had to consciously tell herself to quit thinking about it, to block the "what ifs," to block the variety of scenarios swimming about in her head. She knew she wasn't going to immediately be given the answers, so worrying about it was pointless and futile.

Just breathe, she chided to herself again.

***

A little while later, Alva walked back into the living room, wearing a pair of slacks and an oversized sweater. It looked odd on her, as if she looked too dressed up for someone of her character.

"Well, what do you think?" Alva asked. "How do I look? Like I'm ready for company?"

Lark cleared her throat and took another deep breath. "Sure, you look just fine."

"Fine?" Alva interjected. "I wanna look more than just fine."

"You look . . . great," Lark said, this time forcefully as if trying to convince her own self that this was the truth.

"Oh, good!" Alva clasped her hands together in front of her. "I want to look my best, and with the food smelling delicious, the grandkids won't be disappointed!"

Lark smiled warmly. *I do hope so,* she thought. "Ms. Alva, may I please take a bath or shower or something? Even if I don't have any clothes necessarily to change into . . . at the very least I'd like to feel a bit cleaner than what I do."

Alva bit her lip, her eyebrows furrowed. She hurried down the hallway, leaving Lark to remain seated on the couch. Upon returning, she held an old gray dress in her hands, still dangling from the clothes hanger. "Well, what about this? Looks like your size!" Alva said excitedly.

Oh my gosh, Lark said to herself, watching Ms. Alva parade about with the dress, seemingly unaware of the disgusted look on Lark's face. "Um . . . hmm . . . " Lark said aloud, trying to think of what to say without hurting Ms. Alva's feelings again.

"It's OK," Alva said, patting Lark on the shoulder. "No need to thank me. Just put this on and don't worry that it doesn't match your shoes; they will never notice."

"Ugh," Lark said under her breath, grimacing as she tried to smile. She took the dress from Ms. Alva's hand and walked down the hallway to the bathroom. Walking in and shutting the door, Lark looked around instantly, feeling claustrophobic; the wallpaper seemed to close in on her. She pulled back the shower curtain partway. A yellow line marked the middle of the bathtub, and some rust trickled from the faucet. "That's so disgusting," Lark said, her stomach churning. The idea of sitting in the dilapidated tub unsettled her, but the idea of staying dirty bothered her worse. *Wonder if I can just take a shower?* she thought. She began to remove layer upon layer of clothes until she was fully unclothed and standing alone before a mirror that also looked like it hadn't been cleaned in years.

Gritting her teeth, she pulled back the remainder of the shower curtain until it was pushed back completely, allowing her to step in and pull the shower curtain back across the length of the bathtub, careful not to touch the sides of the tub itself. The water poured from the faucet after Lark turned the knobs, checking to see if the water was clean and half expecting it not to be. Much to her relief, it trickled out clear and warm, so she turned the handle a little further, sending a warm stream of water out. She adjusted it so that the shower spurted less, and then a steady stream fell on her head, back, and hands, causing her to close her eyes. At least it was something, and if she closed her eyes, she could transport herself mentally to her own bathroom and amongst her own things.

Moments passed while Lark continued to let the water beat down against her skin. As it started to cool down, she bent down and adjusted the knob again so that more warmth flowed through. Again, she closed her eyes, whisking herself back to a time when she sat all alone, oblivious to anything or anyone like this.

"Help me, God," Lark said, grabbing a bar of soap that sat on a lonely ledge and rubbing it between her hands, forming a rich lather. "I don't know what You want me to do. Help me to know . . . show me, please. I'm so confused."

Lark rubbed the lather over her and let the water pour back down, rinsing her off in a warm cascade of water droplets. The water now, despite her turns of the knob, was cooling more and more rapidly. Stepping out after she had rinsed off, she glanced around for a towel to dry herself. Once she finished, she hung the towel across the top of the shower bar and gathered up her dirty clothes in a pile. The dress smelled like moth balls, so she held her breath as she slipped it over her head and pulled it the rest of the way down over her thin frame. It was a little big but nothing that was too obvious. Even the fact that it was terribly outdated didn't bother her as much as the smell did.

Lark opened the cabinets under the small sink directly underneath the mirror, looking for anything that might help reduce such a pungent smell, but only a plunger, a couple of rolls of toilet paper, and bottles of cleaning products greeted her.

Guess she forgot she had this cleaning stuff down here, Lark said to herself a bit sarcastically, thinking about the tub. *Oh well,* Lark continued to muse as she frowned and shut the cabinet door quietly. She didn't see much in the way of helpful smells or perfumes, so gathering her dirty clothes up from the pile she had created, she exited the bathroom.

Ms. Alva spotted her and urged her to make her way to the laundry room where Lark put her clothes in the washing machine and called out to Alva if she could start the load. "Yes, that would be fine. Detergent is in the cabinet overhead, directly above the washing machine. Just use it sparingly though, if you don't mind. I'm about out and am not going to town until next week."

Lark answered her politely in agreement and opened the cabinet doors directly above as Ms. Alva had indicated. Only pouring a small amount into the washer as she had been instructed to do, she closed the lid, and the washer hummed to life with the pouring of water into the agitator and then the slow and steady slosh as it moved to and fro. Lark began to close the cabinet but eyed a small, discolored box of dryer sheets with the words, "Mountain Fresh," written underneath its brand. *Hmm . . .* she thought, quickly grabbing the box. Pulling a few sheets out, she sniffed them to see if they were still with their fragrance and not dried out. Sure enough, they were still good. Lark took each one and rubbed them across the dress she was wearing until every square inch had been rubbed with the dryer sheets—though there was still a faint scent of moth balls. The simple idea and marked results made Lark smile, pleased with herself and her ingenuity. *Take that.*

"Ooh . . . now that looks great, and my how good you smell," Alva said. Lark bit her lip, trying her best to keep from telling her what she had done to evoke something that smelled bearable. "Glad that the dress fit." Alva motioned for Lark to follow her as she walked toward the kitchen. "You want something for lunch before you help me tidy up? There's some sandwich meat in the fridge."

"That sounds good, Ms. Alva." Though Lark's stomach was in knots, and the idea of eating anything in light of knowing why she was there just didn't lend its way to a healthy appetite. But if she was going to participate in the family meal later, then she needed to be prepared.

After lunch, Alva gave Lark some chores she could do around the house in order to prepare for the guests' imminent arrival. Taking a break to switch the laundry she had started, she continued to sweep the floor, put away dishes, and fold the blankets draped across the couch from the night before.

"Do you want me to help you set the table for dinner, Ms. Alva?" Lark asked, noticing the time. Their guests would be arriving very soon.

Alva paused for a moment. "Yes, that would be great. I'll show you where the silverware and plates are. I'm just used to them all helping themselves, but it would probably be nice to do something a little different considering the fact they have never met you, and I'll be curious to see if you can weasel your way out of their questioning like you have been doing with me. Difference is, I am OK with a little privacy, and I respect yours like I want others to respect mine."

Lark smiled appreciatively. She finished gathering the plates and silverware from Ms. Alva, brought them to the table, and began laying them out appropriately in an orderly fashion. It reminded her of her obligations as a child, instantly flashing back to the smell of her mother's cooking and distant memories of setting the table for her parents and herself. It brought tears to her eyes, and she quickly brushed them away. Now was not the time to be emotional.

Within moments, Lark heard the familiar rumble of a motor. Her heart skipped a beat, and she struggled to breathe. *Calm down,*

Lark scolded herself and sat down at the head of the table, instantly feeling a bit faint.

"Everything OK?" Ms. Alva asked, taking off her apron and looking at Lark in concern.

"Yes, why do you ask?"

"Because you are as pale as a ghost, that's why."

"Oh, I'm fine," Lark replied, her face suddenly becoming flushed with embarrassment.

A knock at the door made Alva quickly dismiss their conversation as she hurriedly walked to the front door to greet her family.

Lark waited patiently by the table but had stood up in order to greet the people she believed were going to be changed forever.

"Grandma!" a young voice bellowed.

"Joseph, I saw you on the news. I'm so proud!"

"Oh, it was nothing," he said, his face beaming with pride. After hugging his grandma, his eyes scanned the room and fell upon the image of Lark. "Who are you?" he asked, removing his arms from Alva and turning directly toward Lark.

"I'm . . . I'm Lark." Her voice faltered a bit, thinking about his smiling face in the newspaper.

"What are you doing here though?" he continued, questioning.

Lark felt as if she were being interrogated. "Well, it's kinda a weird thing, but I met your grandmother, Ms. Alva, and she invited me to join your family for dinner, if that's OK. I'm from the city."

"Well, where's your car?" he asked.

"I don't have one," Lark stated very matter-of-factly.

"Then, how did you get here?" he continued with a sense of disbelief. Or was that suspicion? Lark couldn't tell.

As her daughter and granddaughter approached the front door and entered the living room, Alva saw them immediately but interjected, "That's too many questions for now, and my food is getting cold. So quit wasting time needling people and let's eat. We can talk more at the table."

Lark continued to watch Ms. Alva's family walk toward the dining table and sit down.

"Hello," Alva's daughter answered, "I'm Abigail Williams. This is my daughter, Sophie, and my son, Joseph. I didn't catch your name."

"Lark."

"Lark?" she said, obviously waiting for a last name.

"Just Lark."

"Hmm, well I was just asking because I might know your parents."

"No," Lark replied, "there's no way you do."

"And why is that?" Mrs. Abigail asked, scooting her chair up and placing her hands in her lap.

"Because they're dead." Lark bit her lip as a hush fell upon the room. She was instantly sorry for having stated such a thing so blatantly. She was just tired of the probing questions and the inquisitive stares, and without knowing what she could or couldn't say, everything was becoming frustrating. The angel had not discussed any of this with her or the ever-growing discomfort and uneasiness that had settled in the room. It was a different kind of atmosphere altogether.

What she really wanted at the moment was to blink her eyes— or something along those lines—and be back in her room in her own home with no one to disturb her or badger her with the auspice of collecting information.

The silence still loomed for a little while longer, but Alva was the first to break it.

"Well, no wonder you didn't say much, child. I think we've had enough seriousness for one day. Everyone grab your plates and follow me into the kitchen to put some good food on 'em. I didn't just do all this for nothing." And with that, Alva rose from the table and grabbed her plate with a look of determination on her face. Everyone began looking at one another, so Lark grabbed hers and followed in turn. Soon everyone else was marching in line toward the kitchen. One by one they poured a heaping helping of Ms. Alva's delicious cooking onto their plates. Lark brought her plate to the table and sat down, waiting for the others. Alva sat down next at the other end of the table, and soon Joseph, Sophie, and Mrs. Abigail also sat down in turn.

As they started eating, Lark spoke: "Think we should have a blessing?" Everyone's eyes looked at her and they sheepishly put down their eating utensils.

"Sure," Alva said, "that would be just fine. Don't think we've done that since my husband passed away. Who's gonna lead us?"

"I will," Lark said, noticing that everyone else seemed to be staring at their plates and not interjecting a desire to do so. "Everyone please close your eyes and bow your heads." With that, Lark began to recite the blessing her parents had taught her so many years ago. She ended by saying "Amen," and everyone raised their heads to resume eating. Though no one said anything, the atmosphere had instantly become less hostile.

Alva was lively and kept wanting to hear all about the state championship, how good the team had to be to get there, the plays, the score, and finally the trophy. Her eyes danced as she listened to her grandson, Joseph, describe the play-by-play action. Everyone else simply listened in amazement at how close the team had actually come through their season to not actually qualifying and almost losing in the play-offs to their most serious rival, the Longview Pirates. Lark was also impressed by Joseph's tenacity and talent like the others, and she was no longer feeling as if the emphasis was on her. Rather, there was joint camaraderie at such a young and gifted athlete.

"Do you think it was televised?" Ms. Alva asked as Joseph finished.

"Oh, yes, Granny . . . they are still showing reruns at the school. It's like no one can believe we really won, and that's all they are talking about these days. It still feels like a dream to me. I'm thinking I'm gonna pinch myself and then wake up."

Lark cleared her throat, his words echoing in her own mind.

"Well, we are all so very proud of you," Alva said. "How are you, Sophie?" she inquired. Ms. Alva tried to include her in the conversation, but Sophie did not seem very interested in talking. "Oh, come on, what's going on?"

"Oh, I know!" Joseph interjected. "She's got a new boyfriend," he said, as if it was his duty to inform everyone.

"Oh, shut up, Joseph. Maybe I do and maybe I don't. I think that's my business and not yours."

Lark tried not to giggle as Sophie blushed, though Sophie tried to pass it off as nothing.

"Well, I was about your age when I had my first suitor," Alva stated.

"Suitor? What's that?" Sophie asked.

"Well," Alva said, rather indignantly, "that's what they called guys who wanted to court, or as y'all say nowadays, *date*, a girl."

"Granny, you are so old-fashioned," Sophie said, her face continuing to blush.

"Oh man, look how red your face is getting!" Joseph belted out in Sophie's direction. Everyone began to chuckle, making Lark feel more relaxed as the conversation continued. This was a sweet and dear little family, even if she didn't know too much about them.

"So . . ." Alva said, after the laughter and uproar of Sophie's new love interest died and she had exhausted the story of Joseph's championship. She looked to Abigail, her face getting serious. "Tell me why Darnell is not here with you and the kids."

"Oh, Mom . . . you know how he is. He goes and does what he wants, and he is probably still fishing," Abigail said. She let her eyes gaze down at her plate as she twirled her fork on her empty plate.

"Well, that's up to you," Alva said with a look of distaste. "Frankly, I wouldn't put up with it."

"Mom!" Abigail said, shocked. "Please don't. Now is not the time."

Alva's face softened, and she looked around the table as if she were studying their faces. "You are right," she said and put her fork to her mouth, taking a bite.

After swallowing a few more bites, Alva chimed into the conversation with more accolades of Joseph's performance and then about her garden and how greatly she missed having it to tend to. Winter was just getting started, and she was ready for it to be over. Lark chuckled to herself, still on pins and needles, but trying her best to relax, engage in conversation, and have a good time.

Had she forgotten why she was there, a part of her would have longed to not leave. To stay and have the human interaction with others that for so long she had been deprived of was a secret desire.

How her heart ached thinking of all the years without a word to others unless it was a perfunctory thing.

Just then the telephone rang, and Lark felt her heart beat faster. Alva, seemingly surprised, stood up from the table to go answer it.

"Hello?" she said into the receiver.

"Alva?" a man's voice replied.

"Yes, Darnell," Alva stated, rolling her eyes and not making any attempt to hide it.

"Alva, I need to talk to Abigail. Can you give her the phone please?"

Alva continued to contort her face but handed the phone to Abigail.

"Darnell, what's going on?" Abigail's voice sounded concerned, nervous. It was unlike him to call.

Although Lark couldn't hear the entire conversation, the obvious signs of distress were unmistakable as Abigail tried to wipe away the tears that began to fall from her eyes. Her hands cupped her head, softly shaking and alarming everyone there.

"Mom?" Joseph said as he put his hand on her shoulder, his eyes full of worry.

"Not now, baby . . . not now."

"Mom, you are scaring me, what's going on? Is it Dad?" he continued.

"Yeah, Mom, what is going on?" Sophie asked, now also inquiring as to what had transpired that was so bad that her mom was suddenly crying. The atmosphere was no longer filled with laughter.

Abigail finally hung up the phone as everyone waited with bated breath. She quickly brushed away the remaining tears in her eyes and slowly turned toward Joseph.

His eyes were sad, worried, anxious.

Lark wanted to say something, but even she did not know what to say, never expecting to hear the words that ensued.

Turning to Joseph, Abigail let out a deep breath before looking into Joseph's eyes as she said sadly, "Your dad received some terrible news earlier. Your best friend was killed in a car accident this morning by a drunk driver. I'm so, so sorry, baby."

Grief Unabated

"W HAT!?" Joseph said angrily, now his own eyes streaming with tears. "That's not right . . . you're lying. That can't be . . . we just talked last night! Mom, please . . . not Grant . . . please . . . oh, please!" His fists slammed onto the table. "This is *not* happening. This is some sort of joke!"

"Oh, honey," Abigail said, trying to comfort him, "I wish it was, honey. I would never say something like this if it wasn't true."

"No! It must be a mistake. Somebody got it wrong," Joseph exclaimed as he moved his hands frantically through his pockets to find his phone. "I will call Grant myself," he insisted, tears continuing to fall down his face.

The phone rang on the other end of the line . . . once . . . twice . . . and then a third time. Joseph was about to hang up when a woman's voice finally answered.

"Mrs. Turner? Can I talk to Grant? It's real important." The phone was silent, followed by the long, audible sobbing of a woman, who Lark could only ascertain was his mother.

Lark could feel the tears welling in her own eyes as she sat like everyone else, still in shock and full of questions. *Why didn't you send me back to save him, God?* Lark thought.

After only a moment, the phone slipped out of Joseph's trembling hands and down to his side, his whole body convulsing with grief. His entire family tried to console him, but it seemed futile. Lark knew all too well the pain, the anger, and the unanswered questions that still loomed, that feeling of helplessness, hopelessness. How her heart ached with him, but she could do nothing. Any efforts to console him would make her true identity an issue.

He fought to maintain some composure, but the anger and hurt was unbearable. He kept slamming his fists on the table, the silverware rattling each time his fist connected with its surface.

Joseph managed to mumble unintelligible words that Lark strained to decipher but could not. His mother tried to wipe at his tears, but he simply pushed her away, too distraught to even care about anything other than his best friend. Even Alva was crying when he began moaning, as if his very heart had been torn from him, an invisible pain only felt by him and yet witnessed by all.

Lark tried her best to simply look on, but the emotional turmoil was so raw, so real, and her own heart broke as she was made privy to this. For once, she felt kindred to him, a compassion she had never known with anyone. She feared showing emotions, afraid of them because it might expose her to feeling and caring for others, and she had refused to ever be that way again.

So why was this happening? Was she allowing herself to care? What good would it do, knowing she had some mission to accomplish and then she was gone, never to return? It hardly seemed fair.

Joseph finally agreed to go sit on the couch. His mother took the phone from his hands and went into the kitchen to talk to Grant's mother and make a few other phone calls. Joseph watched her but said nothing. His sister sat beside him, and Alva instructed him to calm down and encouraged him that everything would be OK.

"No, Granny, everything's not OK," he replied, wiping his nose and staring back at her with his piercing blue eyes. "My best friend is dead. Somebody killed him. They took him away from me, and I want him back."

"But you can't, Joseph," Alva replied as tenderly as she could.

"Well, maybe I should just go to him then," he said matter-of-factly.

His words caused Lark to look up and at him more intently. Had his family heard that? Were they thinking what she was? Did he intend to harm himself? Or was it just the grief playing games with his head? She couldn't be too sure, but a strong sense came over her that something was going to happen, and very soon. She needed to watch his every move.

Alva didn't seem to be as alarmed by his comment, and it was obvious when she responded by telling him that wouldn't be possible and that he would see him in heaven when God decided. She told him not to worry, that Grant was a Christian and he was in a much better place.

But by this time, Joseph had a different demeanor altogether. He was quiet and pensive, the tears weren't flowing as much, and his hands had stopped shaking. Alva and Sophie seemed happier at his mannerisms, as if he was starting to relax, but in the pit of Lark's stomach she felt an unsettling feeling that, despite her efforts, she could not shake off. She was sure it was him in the picture. Positive that it was his mother who had stumbled and fallen out of the grocery store. She was absolutely convinced now that the beautiful girl sitting beside him as his sister was none other than the angry, gothic cashier who had checked her out just recently. She just couldn't shake the question, *What led them to that?*

Joseph's mom was still quietly speaking in the kitchen. From time to time, she would look toward the living room and then whisper back into the receiver. Finally she hung up the phone, walked back into the living room, and sat on the couch with the others.

Lark had remained at the table, not wanting to be rude but also out of respect because she was not family.

"Well, I don't know if you are capable of hearing more, but I spoke to your father again and he had heard some more information about what happened," Abigail continued. "But I don't want to overwhelm you any further than what you are. You just let me know when you wanna talk, and we will."

"I wanna know NOW, Mom!" he demanded, looking up at her, his eyes pleading for answers.

"It was an underage, intoxicated driver. Seems that Grant's family had been out celebrating the victory of the state championship, and a truck veered out in front of their SUV and struck the side that Grant was sitting on. Their car flipped and rolled into the median. Your dad told me that even though the medics were there quickly, along with law enforcement, Grant had already passed away. All the other family members were bruised, and I think his sister, Meaghan, suffered a broken arm. They were checked out and released by the hospital physicians." Abigail paused, letting her words sink in and gauging the expression on her son's face for signs of understanding. While a few tears did fall, he remained motionless. She continued by telling him that though nothing was definite, it appeared it would be a closed casket for the visitation the following day, with the funeral to proceed shortly thereafter. Joseph didn't say anything, the only movement being a simple nod.

Lark felt at a loss, still sitting at the table. Was there something she should do? Something she should say?

Alva offered everyone to simply stay the night, and Abigail agreed that would be best.

It still felt so strange, preparing the pallets for bed and everyone taking baths. All in silence, no one contributing a word. No one knowing what to say. Lark closed her eyes and prayed as her turn to take another shower arrived. Grateful to finally be alone, the grief almost unbearable, she stood as the water poured over her head and trickled in large rivulets down her arms and legs. She closed her eyes, now letting her own tears fall.

What would you have me do? Why have you sent your angel to bring me to a place where only pain exists? Have I not suffered enough? Lark formed the words upon her quivering lips, but no audible voice was heard. *How in the world do you expect me to fix anything here? Shouldn't I have been given my chance to save the other boy? I don't understand.* Her feelings of hurt turned to anger.

Despite her desire to remain transfixed in the shower and not be disturbed, the water quickly went cold as it had earlier that morning, and Lark could not stay underneath it any longer.

She studied herself in the mirror, her eyes glistening with tears, still stinging and red. "OK, so now what?" she said aloud, though she didn't expect an answer. She figured she would just go ahead and put on the same clothes as she had been found in, since she had put them in the washer, and she didn't really want to wear the dress any longer. It was a good thing she had found them since Ms. Alva tended to move things around frequently, and in the given situation, it might have left her in nothing more than her birthday suit. "Ugh," Lark said, picking up the clothes and putting them to her nose. *Perhaps Ms. Alva forgot to dry them,* Lark thought, but could not be sure. They smelled musty, and it repulsed her as she slowly separated them out and put them back on. She was surprised that no one had mentioned her staying as well, but with everything else going on, perhaps they had simply held in their feelings regarding the matter, as other more important matters had taken precedence.

The living room and hallway were dark when she exited, and it took a few moments for her eyes to adjust so that she could move forward without running the risk of stepping on anyone or waking anyone up.

Quietly, she tiptoed, her hands pressed against the side of the hallway for added support. Everything was quiet, and she wasn't sure of where she needed to go. She figured that Joseph had been given the couch, so hopefully she was at the very least somewhere far enough away that she could think and not be stared at through the night. She continued to fumble her way around the back of the living room furniture until, thanks to the moonlight flickering through the blinds, she noticed a solitary sleeping bag near the dining table. *Perfect,* she thought. She headed that way and lay down.

It was by no means comfortable, but she was glad for whatever kind gesture was extended to her. It was difficult to be still; her mind raced and her heart quickened with a sense of dread. The shadows played tricks in her head as she stared at the walls, forcing herself to relax. Before too long, she had dozed off, the emotional roller-coaster now having dwindled, leaving everyone exhausted and emotionally drained. However, a strong, cold breeze forced her eyelids to open, and a voice whispered in her ear, "Lark, it's time. Awake!"

Lark sat upright in her sleeping bag, not sure how long she had been in slumber and half expecting to see the angel looming in front of her. But it was pitch black. She quietly got out of the sleeping bag and began to tiptoe around Abigail and Sophie, knowing that Alva was probably in her own bedroom. The only other place to check was the couch. She was sure that's where Joseph had lay down. What if she touched him and he woke up? She could just about imagine the lights turning on and everyone looking at her like some sort of alien. But as she slowly eased closer to where he should have been lying, her fears were confirmed. He was gone!

Lark began to panic as she moved her hands across the couch to see if he had simply moved to one side, but only the blanket was left. She moved toward the hallway but it was also dark, no light on in the bathroom. Where could he be? She tried to reason but nothing came to mind. *Maybe he went out for a walk,* she thought. Maybe that's why she had felt that cold breeze. She made her way back to where she had been sleeping and put her shoes on and the thick parka that lay alongside her. She wished she had a flashlight, but there was no time for that now. Gently, she eased open the latch and exited the front door, making sure to close it back softly. The wind cut like a knife, and Lark stuck her hands into her pockets to keep them warm. *Now what?*

She stood alone on the porch. She could see a good distance due to the illumination of the moon, but though she scanned her perimeter, nothing seemed out of the ordinary. And then she heard a sound. It was ever so faint but definitely a man-made sound. She stepped off the porch and began running toward it. About half of a mile away, in the far right of the property, stood a pair of massive trees whose limbs seemed like gigantic fingers, reaching toward the heavens. She wasn't sure what was going on, but she knew deep within that she needed to hurry.

With every step she ran, her breathing intensified. The gusts of air blew back in her face like smoke having cooled so quickly in the icy weather. Her toes had already begun feeling numb, as well as her fingertips. She didn't know if he was watching her or not, and she didn't care. As she neared the trees, she tried to scan the area for him. But despite straining, she didn't see him around the base of the trees. She ran frantically around them and paused.

Another sound broke the silence; it was coming from overhead. Lark looked up. There on one of the tree branches stood Joseph. He was shivering and holding on to a piece of rope that he seemed to be struggling to get around his neck. "Oh my, oh no!" Lark whispered to herself. He was going to kill himself.

"Joseph!" Lark screamed at the top of her lungs. "Don't do this, please!"

Joseph didn't seem to be moved at all by Lark's desperate pleas. Continuing to still fumble with the rope to make sure it was tight, he appeared robotic in his demeanor, void of emotion.

"Please, Joseph," Lark said, trying to see if she could climb up the tree in time. "This isn't the way, I promise. Just listen to me for a second . . . just a second!"

"What do you want?" he responded angrily.

"Why are you doing this? Nothing will bring him back."

"I know that," he said sardonically, "that's why I'm going to be with him."

"This isn't the way, Joseph . . . you are making a mistake. Trust me."

"Trust you? I don't even know who the heck you are or why you are even here," he said, staring down at her as she paced to and fro under the branch he stood on.

"I know you don't," Lark said, fighting back tears, "but I was sent here for you."

"Me? Ha!" he said in disbelief.

"It's true, I really was, and I don't know if I'm supposed to tell you that or not, but I really am. You have to believe me that your purpose here is not finished. That this will only bring more pain and more hurt for years and years to come."

"I don't care," he said, shrugging his shoulders, "but even if I did, how do you know that?"

Lark could barely feel her fingertips anymore. She tried to stuff them back into her pockets, but they were still cold, so she tried to bring them both to her mouth to breathe on them and rub them together feverishly. "I've seen it, that's why. And if you come down from there, I'll tell you everything I know. But I can't do it from here; I'm about to turn into a popsicle as it is."

"You don't know anything," he replied, his teeth chattering as he spoke.

"Well, try me then. I've got nothing better to do."

Joseph seemed alarmed at Lark's defiance and resilience. She was aware that deep down he knew that this wasn't the right course, but grief had set in and clouded sound judgment as she knew all too well. Many times, she had been in the depths of despair and struggled against the force that would have her think of such a decision, especially since she was alone, no one to tend to her, no one to miss her, and yet always in her own sad state. A small voice would say, "Get up, stand tall, fight on." For many months, she would struggle with this maxim. Then as time went by, it became her motto, a saying for painful days to strengthen her and remind her that she had been left on the earth for something greater than herself. That despite her pain and loss, she was greater than the situation that had presented itself. For just as a day could be cloudy and melancholy, on others, rays of sunshine would appear, reminding her to persevere another hour, another day, another year.

"Joseph, I know how badly you hurt. I wish I could take it away, but I can't, and I wasn't sent here to save your friend or bring him back either. I have no control of that or anything else for that matter. But I'm pleading with you from the bottom of my heart to please get down and talk with me."

"I don't believe you," he uttered, still shivering. "The minute I get down, you are gonna go run to my mom and she's gonna send me to some mental institution and everyone is gonna make fun of me. I want to be with my friend and that's all there is to it. Don't you understand anything?" he said, his voice choking as he spoke.

Lark wasn't sure if he was crying or not, but she knew he was in too fragile a state to keep arguing with him. Something else needed to be done, perhaps a different approach. But what?

"I'm not gonna say anything to anyone if you promise me to just come down from there. If not, I'm gonna come up there myself and cut you loose or the branch is gonna break with both of us on it and we will just go down together."

"Are you serious?" he said incredulously.

"As a heart attack. Now come down, please, for the last time, Joseph. If you do this, there is no coming back, no chance to change your mind. No matter how sad you are feeling right now, I do not believe your friend would want this for you. He loved life, right? He would want you to live yours, to live it fully, live it freely, as he would have done. You and I both know, as Christians, it's not a good-bye, it's a see you later." Tears streamed down Lark's face as she spoke, quietly praying that the words she uttered would strike a chord within him. Hoping he would listen, that he would spare himself and his family from such a tragic and unnecessary act.

Joseph was quiet as Lark stood frozen. She could feel the snowflakes hitting her face. The tears stinging and quickly drying one by one as she waited for what seemed like an eternity but realistically no more than a few moments. Lark half expected to have to climb the tree, and if he jumped she didn't know what she would do. Unless she knew the exact place he would jump so she could catch him, it was futile. *Please, God, please let him know that he matters to You, that You have great things in store for him, that it's not too late to grasp on to hope.*

Before Lark could finish lifting her head, the sound of rustling leaves and branches filled the air. Lark stood still for fear he would change his mind or was only getting her hopes up. Once down, he turned to face her, their eyes meeting, the rope still in his hand. Lark didn't know whether to say something or not, so she simply reached her half-frozen hands out, extending them toward him. At first, the silence was uncomfortable, but soon he walked to her, surprising her by taking her hands and burying his head into her jacket as he sobbed freely.

"It's OK, Joseph . . . I promise . . . it does get better. You just gotta have faith that each new day brings healing." Lark stood in the wintry breeze as Joseph's sobs now turned to muffled whimpers. She was so cold but needed for Joseph to truly let out his grief, his pain, his mourning. She knew it would take time and perhaps counseling to ease him through such a terrible event in his life, but climbing down from that tree and hugging her now instead of taking his own life was nothing short of a miracle. This could only lead to more positive choices by such a strong and talented boy. The world needed *more* Josephs in it, not less.

"Come on, let's go inside before we freeze. I'll tell you all I know; you decide for yourself." Joseph nodded and walked with Lark, shivering in silence. Lark was no longer tired; she was full of joy and gratefulness. The strength and fragility of life never being so evident to her as it was at the very moment Joseph had stepped down from danger and embraced deliverance. But now what would become of her?

"Joseph, we are gonna have to be real quiet, OK?"

"What? Uh, yeah . . . of course. Did you think I was really gonna go blabbering about everything?"

Lark looked at him. "I know that, I just want you to be quiet and stay with me to talk. I'm absolutely convinced that you are supposed to do something truly amazing and that while your beginnings may be seeped with grief, you need to be strong for those who are still here. Your friend, Grant . . . you are sure he knew God or just knew of Him?"

Choking a little on his tears, he tried to clear his throat before speaking. "He and I used to attend church together. He believed."

"That's good!" Lark said, looking at him with comfort. "What about you?"

"I mean, I know God . . . I know what He did . . . I accepted salvation when I was a kid. I just kinda stopped going to church and stuff after Dad quit taking us. Guess he just got too busy with his own life. He kinda neglected doing much with us after that. It bothers Mom more than it does us though. Sophie and I are used to doing our own thing."

The Consequence

T he rest of the night and into the morning was truly the closest
Lark had ever been to anyone besides her parents. Joseph felt
like the little brother she wished she had in her life. He was a wealth
of knowledge and budding curiosity. Talking until the first rays of
sunlight flirted between the blinds, they hugged one another with a
fervor that each had truly needed but would have never expressed.
Through the grief, tragedy, and despair, a newfound hope and
purpose had emerged, and Lark not only had witnessed it but was
part of it. She felt that he was in a good place. That he would be sad
still for a long time, and maybe, like her, the pain would never go
away, but he now had a healthy way of expressing it and a desire to
return to church—back to restoring what had been lost.

"So you honestly don't know how you got here? I mean the
angel didn't tell you anything?" Joseph asked in amazement.

"Yep, it was surreal. A lot of light and then this place. But you
know our agreement, right?" Lark responded, her eyes boring into his.

"Yeah, I don't tell your story, you don't tell mine. It's a deal.
Besides, sure if I told them yours, I would only get laughs back. It's
not something you hear every day, that's for sure. I dunno . . . I don't
know what to believe. I really was ready to say good-bye. I never
expected you, or anyone for that matter, to find me until it was all

over. I mean, looking back, it was selfish, but I didn't mean for it to be. I was hurting, I'm still hurting, but I know now that it isn't the answer. You did that! You made me see that. Whether I believe all of your fantastic story or not, I thank you."

Lark let a tear escape as she responded, "It wasn't all me, man, and you know it. I was just called and I answered. The ball is in your court now to do something really great with your life. Remember, every day is a gift, so live it like it is." *Good advice for anyone,* Lark thought, *including myself.*

Suddenly a light flickered, then the bright light. Joseph seemed confused, but Lark knew her time with him was over; it was time to go home. A part of her was elated but another feeling also engulfed her: sadness. Now that she had made a friend, she didn't want to let go. But as she and Joseph stared, the light grew brighter and purer until her own eyes closed as they had done mere days before, too bright to stare into and too powerful to resist.

"Thank you," she said, hoping God heard her. "It was good while it lasted." With that, she squeezed Joseph's hand until she felt herself become weightless again. "Bye, my friend . . ." her own voice trailing off as she became as thin as air.

Amiel stood beside Lark as she transitioned back into her time, her place, and her own bedroom. He knew it had been a beautiful thing, as she had bravely stepped into the unknown and another child had been saved from such a senseless tragedy. But now, he had to give her the news he had not disclosed to her before.

"Lark." Amiel's voice was strong, comforting.

Lark's eyes fluttered for a moment as they adjusted. She felt so energized. "A-m-i-e-l," she said slowly, turning her head to face him.

He smiled and it made her smile as well.

"We did it!" Her eyes twinkled. "I have never felt so alive as when he decided to embrace life with me."

"I know," Amiel responded, crouching down to kneel by her bedside.

"What's wrong?" Lark said, sensing a difference in his demeanor.

"Nothing is wrong, it's just that I should have explained a side effect of going back."

"What?" Lark said immediately, sitting upright in the bed, somewhat alarmed at the revelation. "What side effect?" She got out of bed, looking herself up and down, and headed for the mirror, not sure what was happening. "What did you do to me?" her voice now becoming more panicked.

"I did nothing, Lark," he said. "There is no need for your anxiousness. The side effect is simply that as you go back in time, the years that you went back are added to your own life now that you have returned."

"What?"

"I didn't want to alarm you, Lark. You are just fine, just increased in age a bit. Please don't be afraid or alarmed."

"Alarmed?" As soon as Lark said that, she locked eyes upon her reflection in the mirror. She had aged! And not by a few months or even a few years; it was at least ten years, if not more!

"Ahh!!" she screamed. "Why didn't you say anything?"

"Would it have changed your mind? Would you have said no?"

Lark grew quiet as she studied her aged features in the mirror, poking and pinching at her face as if to check resilience. She knew she would have done it all over again, but it was the surprise at such a thing that caught her off-guard and left her pondering everything.

"You know I would have still helped, but I would have liked to know."

"What would it have helped or hurt?" Amiel said, trying to understand the concept of humans.

"It's not that it helps or hurts," Lark said with conviction, "just that I think it was important to tell me everything, you know . . . full disclosure!"

"I didn't know that was a requirement to compassion," he said, standing near the entrance of her room.

Lark looked at him and paused. He did intimidate her, and the conversation was moot and trivial in the grander scheme of things, but exactly how old was she now? Good thing she didn't have anyone to answer to or they would question the obvious changes. A few years in solace and no one would be the wiser.

"OK, you win. It's not like you will change me back, right? So what happens now?" she said, stepping away from the mirror.

"I go home," Amiel said.

"And will I ever see you again?" Lark asked with a forlorn look.

"That, I cannot say. I have only the will of the Father to obey. Where He directs, I go. I have no knowledge that I will be seeing you again, but until I was given this mission, I was not aware of you. So there is always a possibility."

"Yeah, but look at me. You are just gonna leave me here? Do I get to ever find out what happened to that family?" Lark asked, inwardly hoping he would tarry a little longer.

"Lark, of trivial things, I have no inclination. You must continue to live your life and live it sagaciously." Amiel then vanished, leaving her to stand in front of the mirror and look at herself objectively, slowly taking into account what felt or looked different. Her eyes looked older and wiser—but not happier. She was alone again and seemingly without direction. She looked about the house for the paper that once had the picture of Joseph. She remembered it being a type of memoriam and recalled that she had left it in the kitchen. She hurried to its location on the far side of the counter.

Opening it up in a hurry, she went right to the page she knew it had recently been. As she predicted, it was gone, and now an ad for a new car dealership in town had taken its place. Lark breathed a sigh of relief, grateful that the entire picture was now no longer in existence.

She began to make coffee as usual, and though her mind raced as she thought about everything that had recently happened, she did her best to sit back and become acclimated again with her own surroundings and breathe in deeply. How wonderful and fantastical these past few days had been, and yet, there was no one to confide in. It had been a long time since she had been to visit her parents' graves, and while she knew they were not really there in a spiritual sense—nor could they hear her—in times past it felt good to go there, place flowers, and speak to them of her day or other current events. That felt more like therapy than anything. It seemed a good time to go, so Lark donned a pair of shoes, pulled back her hair into a ponytail, and soon was back in her old truck heading to the only cemetery in the town.

It was a quaint one with picturesque oak, willow trees, and angelic statues littered about as if they were silently welcoming the souls of the departed. Her parents were buried on the outskirts in part of the oldest portion of the cemetery, as the family burial lots had been purchased ages ago and thus that one small corner had been dedicated to many of her descendants for decades. A beautiful mausoleum had later been erected about fifty or sixty years before her birth, and that was where her parents' bodies lay in slumber, even if their souls did not. Having arrived and parked, Lark scolded herself as her breathing became more labored with each step. It seemed as if in mere days her strength had diminished, leaving a normally uneventful exercise daunting.

Almost there, she said to herself, looking at the stone structure. It was a truly tranquil setting, especially in light of the fact that no one else was around to ogle at her or inquire as to her purpose. "Ahh . . ." Lark said, sitting down on the stony surface and breathing a final sigh of relief. It had been far too long since she had sat beside their graves and paid her respects.

"Mom, Dad . . . you are never gonna believe what happened to me," Lark began as if she were sitting down with them and having afternoon tea. She regaled meeting Amiel as well as Joseph and his family, and she made sure to account for her unpleasant side effects. Though her words were met with silence, she continued as if her very life depended on sharing each minute detail, until finally, catching her breath, she paused, hung her head down, and reached her hands out to stroke their headstones. It was a gesture she had always done over the years, quietly and slowly tracing their names with the tips of her delicate fingers. Inevitably it would cause her to cry and thus force her to leave when the memories and emotional pain hurt too bad. This time was no different, and as the tears trickled down to dampen the concrete below, she forced herself to stand up and head back toward her truck, sitting for a few minutes before putting the keys in the ignition and traveling back toward the house where a long, hot bath awaited her.

Before long, the sun had set and Lark, despite her attempts to sleep, lay in her pillowy comforters and stared at the ceiling, deep in thought. She wanted to go to town and see if Joseph's sister, Sophie, was still working at the local supermarket. If somehow, some way, perhaps she could see them all again and see what had transpired since Joseph's decision to embrace life instead of running from it, she thought that might lift her spirits.

But deep down inside, she knew that if she were recognized, it would bring a flurry of questions, ones she would not want to answer. *Best to just leave people alone,* she thought. Isn't that how she wanted people to treat her? Let her exist in peace and quiet?

Softly, she repeated the Lord's Prayer and closed her eyes. Soon, a new day would dawn, and it would be back to her projects around the house to keep her mind and body preoccupied.

The house itself was still pretty well straightened from her last couple of cleanings, so with a little gusto she would tackle the floor of the main hallway and perhaps begin painting one of the large guest bedrooms. "Yes," she said quietly with a smile on her lips as if she was pleased with her plans. Slowly but surely she drifted off to sleep.

When morning came, her resolve seemed a bit diminished, and her efforts to get up early and begin her projects laid by the wayside as she put one leg over the other and eased her way out of bed only to discover it was already past noon.

Ugh, she scolded herself and began getting dressed. Before long though, she had moved the materials she needed to where she would begin, and, stopping to drink a couple of cups of coffee, she set out to accomplish what she could.

***

After dark, she finally put away the last of the paintbrushes and headed down the hallway to get cleaned up and call it a day. Though the work had been plentiful and tedious, she couldn't help but allow her thoughts to linger on Joseph. What had he done with his life? Would she see him one day and he hug her, or would he even remember? Maybe he wouldn't say a word, just as they had promised one another. Guess it didn't really matter. What was done was done, and she had never felt more exhilaration in her life in those few days.

For the next few weeks, she pulled out her journal and wrote in it as the mood struck her, and other days she would complete various projects around the house to keep her mind preoccupied.

It had initially felt odd coming back to her place and being alone again, even after such a short glimpse into communion with others. But gradually this dissipated, and she was once again her usual self, alone, reserved, and if anything, a bit wiser than she had been.

The house projects had come along nicely, and as the weeks turned to months, Lark hunkered down during the cold ones with the anticipation of beginning repairs to the outside of the property once the early signs of spring began to show. It was welcoming from a rather harsh winter, and as the flowers began to bud and blossom on the dogwood trees, she sat back eager to get started, no longer satisfied being cooped up in her abode. Even if it was capacious, nothing beat fresh open air and space. It was as if flora and fauna both opened their eyes and awakened to gloriousness. *What an interesting and truly beautiful world we live in,* she mused.

She continued to read the daily paper delivered each day for the current events and for any sign of the family she had been introduced to, but there wasn't any trace of them, despite her meticulous review of each article.

Soon months led to a few years passing, and the journal began to irritate her instead of bring her joy. The same old, same old was written over and over again. Though some of it still contained her hopes and aspirations, sadly her life and movements were as repetitious as the clock on the wall. *Ticktock* went the clock; *ticktock* went her life. She was proud that she had made efforts to smile more and make it a point to purposely greet and shake hands with those she came into contact with on her trips to town, but nothing more had changed. She still had no visitors except for a sweet couple of elderly women who had knocked on her door right before the holidays and invited her to church.

"There's a Christmas cantata," one of the ladies had chimed in after saying hello. "You'd really like it."

"I'll think about it," Lark had said, sticking her hand out politely and grabbing the program they offered. She knew it was a lie, even if she thought it was nice and appreciated the gesture. The idea of being around that many people had become terrifying.

Why can't I just be normal? she thought, closing the door after the women had quietly stepped down from the porch and drove away. Moments like that made her more frustrated than anything, maybe even as strong as anger toward herself. It had been so long since she had truly laughed and played that this—whatever this was—had become the new normal for her, even if in everyone else's eyes, it was not.

Just take another bath, she chided herself, *everything will be fine. You will get out there one day.* But Lark knew those words were nothing more than a fictitious joke, no matter how encouraging she tried to tell herself that it was.

The nightmares had returned as well, this time with a vengeance and causing her to awaken to the sound of her own voice screaming in the silence, her body drenched in sweat. Those were the worst—when she wanted to continue screaming as she sat upright in bed. Just when she thought she was finally starting to get better, now a nasty relapse had sent her spiraling into despair again. And then as time wore on, the emotional sunshine would reappear, and she would tackle another project or venture into town and relax a little around all those she tried so hard during the darker days to avoid. Telling herself to take one day at a time.

On one of those particular outings, she could have sworn she saw Joseph's sister, Sophie, but Lark wasn't completely sure. She looked like her from what she remembered, but the hair was light and her face happy, without all the dark makeup. She dressed like she worked in an office or some other nice place—no sign of black and gothic clothing at all. She wanted to chase the young woman down and ask her what her name was, but she was too nervous, despite the strong urge to follow her and inquire as to her identity. For so long after the initial encounter, she thought it had been best to avoid them, thinking it wasn't good to be recognized. Now, she wasn't so sure. What was truly wrong with her not finding out if they were OK and that their lives had gone on and had been successful? Or maybe they hadn't, and maybe her stepping out of her world and into theirs had been a huge mistake.

No, their lives were for the better, she knew it. She sensed it in her heart. That's why Amiel had come back for her, to take her home. The mission had been accomplished.

Strangely enough, the few strands of gray hair didn't bother her now. Every time she would look in the mirror, they were like a badge of honor. A bittersweet reminder that she had done something good and purposeful with her life. That it had mattered. For so long, she had envied all those who came home to someone, something, and that was their world. However, had she not been in the very particular situation she was in, she might not have been chosen for such a cause. *Guess it really is true that everything happens for a reason,* she thought, *even when you don't know why.*

But now what? How could she overcome her own battles in order to continue living with such a mindset? She knew it was unhealthy to keep living the way she had been, but how could she change? She had completed all her projects, read every book in the house, and amassed things that had soon lost their luster. If God had seen her and sent Amiel, could He not see her now? Why didn't He intervene?

"Oh, I get it," she uttered loudly as if speaking to Him, "You want ME to do it, huh? Well, I've tried, and I just can't seem to dig myself out of this emotional grave I've either been thrust in or laid in, so what now? You sent me back to save Joseph, but what about me? I'm hurting . . . I need—"

She stopped mid-sentence, not sure if talking like that was such a good idea. When she had been little and her parents had taken her to church, she had always been a little timid or afraid of God. Maybe it wasn't such a good idea to try to argue with Him. Amiel had been huge, and he was simply one among hundreds of thousands, maybe millions, of angelic beings. She shuddered for a moment, feeling contrite about the outburst.

Lark fell to her knees. "Look, God, I'm sorry, OK? I just don't understand, that's all. You have me help someone, and then You bring me back for what? What do You want me to do? You take me back in time to save him, but why don't You save me?" Lark spoke aloud, letting her voice echo, the silence resonating louder than her own cry and frustrating her to the point of tears.

The wooden planks were hurting her knees, but she didn't feel like standing. "Why won't You let me know? You love me, right?" She put her head down and cupped her face with her hands.

Just then, Lark felt the warmth and light that now she was no longer afraid of. "AMIEL!" she exclaimed as the light grew brighter and a form emerged.

Amiel smiled as Lark stayed kneeling, droplets of joy streaming. He was happy to see her again and could feel her despair begin to dissipate in his presence.

"Lark, peace be with you."

"Amiel, why haven't you come to visit me sooner?"

"Lark, you know that I can't do that, or at least you should, as I am only allowed to come when I am instructed to do so."

"So He heard me, did He?" Lark said as she stood upright and brushed the dirt off her knees from the floor where she had recently knelt.

"He always hears, Lark. You must dismiss this notion that He doesn't care, understand, or listen. Why do you still doubt that?"

"I just wish there was more that I was able to do, more . . . that I could do," Lark replied sadly.

"What makes you think that you cannot? You are a daughter of the King. Don't you see how beautiful of a creation you are?"

Another Soul

U m . . . not really."

"Then, Lark, you need to be reminded about who you really are, because you clearly have been blinded with sadness for far too long. Did it please you to help Joseph?"

"Immensely," Lark responded. "But something tells me that you know that already. So why ask me?"

"To see if you would admit it aloud to yourself."

"Well, I did. So what happens now?" Lark laughed, the sound of it foreign to her.

"Would you be willing if you were given the chance to save another?" Amiel spread his wings wider and looked down at her intently.

"Maybe . . . ?" Lark said, looking back.

Amiel stared at her, "Maybe?"

"OK," Lark said exhaling, "I would, but will it be like last time?"

"What are you asking?"

"Will it be, you know, someone like Joseph? Honestly, I didn't think for a minute that he was gonna come down from that tree. It was terrifying."

Amiel said nothing, seemingly lost in thought.

"Hey," Lark said, "you all right? Were you listening?"

"Oh yes, I am. I am just contemplating what you just said."

"Which part?"

"Does it truly matter what you save a person from, or is it more important that you simply save them?"

Lark bit her lip. He had a point, but seeing Joseph about to commit suicide was the most horrific thing she had ever seen. And then when he came down and they talked for hours afterward—one of the best experiences ever. Was that normal? Did she think she could help someone else without caring, regardless of how it affected her? And if aging before had made this much impact on her body, what would going back another time do? There were so many questions but very few answers. If she was going to help another, then it would simply be an act of faith and trust just as it had been before. Only now, she knew the odds she was up against and the consequences that would remain.

"Can you tell me where and how far back this time? Anything . . . so I'm not fumbling in the dark like before?" Lark said and brushed a few hairs from her face.

"Lark, we have already discussed this. You know I am not given this information and can only disclose what I have been sent to say. I can no more give you answers to your inquiries as before. The choice is yours as it was the first time. Are you willing?"

Lark pondered his words. Her own heart beating rapidly and the feeling of intense dread beginning to overwhelm her.

"Lark," Amiel said, "stop. Do not let fear consume you." His hands reached out to hold her as she stood shaking, her body tense. "You are not obligated to do anything, and you know that. However, just as before, you have this opportunity to make a difference. To step out in *faith* and make an effort to change another's. Having second thoughts now?"

"It's not that," Lark said, as she fidgeted. "I just didn't think it was so much of an emotional roller-coaster. I just don't feel like I'm cut out to do stuff like that."

Amiel put his head down for a moment before responding. "Then, just what are you 'cut out' to do?"

"Well," Lark responded sheepishly, "I'm content to just be here and tend to things as they come along."

"Oh, really, Lark? How's that going for you? Shall I remind you that the Father sees all and knows all? Were that the case, you would have not been on your knees and crying out because of grief, loneliness, and frustration. Do you still not believe that the Father has been carrying you and continues to do so, and will do so just as He always has? What more will it take for you to believe? Does my presence not have any effect?"

Lark bit her lip to pause, Amiel's words dripping with truth. "I do believe you, Amiel, and I don't doubt God. What I doubt is myself."

"Are you not His creation?"

"Yes, but—"

"But what? You think He made a mistake? Think He won't give you everything you need just as He did the time before to complete the task He has set before you? To me, that sounds like you are still doubting Him."

Lark was about to speak but thought better of it. Sure, she could argue back and forth, but it would do no good and he was right, even if she was only brave enough to receive the truth. She wasn't just doubting herself. She was ultimately doubting God by assuming she was not equipped or would be.

"OK, Amiel, you are right, and I can see that now. I will go again. I will try to help someone else if I can."

"I am pleased that you chose wisely."

"And why is that?" Lark said, confused by the comment.

"Is this life not meant to be spent in helping others, exhibiting His love and glorifying Him?"

"Yes, but I'm not contributing to the darkness of the world."

"Not directly, but in a way you are by not extending His light within you and living secluded from the rest of the world."

"But you know how hard it is for me, Amiel!"

"With God, *all* things are possible, Lark! Not a few things or some things, *all* things."

Lark walked into the living room with Amiel following and sat down on the couch.

"Do I go just as before?"

"Yes. Do you feel ready now?" Amiel said, stretching out his wings that were an exquisite thing in and of itself to behold.

"I'm as ready as I will ever be," Lark said, looking once more around the room before breathing in deeply.

Amiel spread his wings further, and the light began to grow brighter and brighter just as before. Lark squinted and stretched out her hands. "Let's go," she told herself, though her heart continued to beat wildly.

The light eventually consumed her warmly in an engulfing wave. But when she opened her eyes, she felt tiny droplets of rain falling on them and running down her face.

"Freezing cold before, now rain?" Lark said quietly. "Why can't I wake up on a beach somewhere?"

It wasn't a heavy downpour, just a slight drizzle that felt more like mist when the wind blew than actual raindrops.

"So where did you bring me now?" Lark muttered rhetorically, wiping her face and glancing upward.

There were buildings all over, and cars whizzed by her at a breakneck pace, no signs of slowing down. Lark kept blinking through the rain as she tried to steady herself from a wave of nausea that made her only want to lie down.

"Ugh . . ." she said, wrapping her arms around her stomach and standing as still as she could, hoping it would pass. When it did not, she heaved until her stomach contents sat in a grotesque clump. Wiping her face, she turned away in disgust. *That was gross,* she thought, trying to figure out why she felt so bad.

The smell lingered and Lark walked away, her stomach still upset and painful but not as badly as before. She seemed to be on a main thoroughfare, gauging from the amount of traffic passing her, and no doubt in some large metropolis with the skyscrapers that loomed in almost every direction, which only served to aid feelings of being overwhelmed.

"Amiel," she said under her breath, "where in the heck am I?" But again it was more of an academic comment and useless, just as the time he had dropped her off to help Joseph and disappeared in the blink of an eye. She knew he wouldn't answer because he wasn't there.

It was still raining, so Lark folded her hands about her and began walking closer to the road to see if she could make out her whereabouts. It wasn't too far of a walk. Nevertheless, she was cautious with every step. The streetlights were playing tricks with her head, as the shadows seemed to dance menacingly through the beams of light. A stray cat meowed in the distance, and entire parking lots sat bare like a ghost town. Terribly uninviting. Lark felt a chill that seemed to go all the way down her spine.

The rain had begun to really pour down, and her hair was now drenched as well as her clothes. The drops of precipitation, despite her attempts to cover her face, managed to stay attached to her eyelashes, making it difficult to see. But she continued to walk toward the traffic.

The lights seemed to no longer appear in sets of two but more like a long blur. Before she knew it, the sound of a horn blared loudly at her, and a man's gruff voice yelled out of his window, "Get out of the way, you idiot!" He pointed at Lark as he continued his ranting with obscenities and his middle finger thrust in her direction.

Lark didn't say a word but backed up a few steps and wiped her eyes as best she could, despite the outpour of heavenly tears. The man rolled up his window and continued moving, though Lark wasn't sure if it was because he was finished interjecting his foul language or because all the other vehicles were all on their horns behind him and proceeding to be as rude to him as only seconds before he had been to her.

Serves him right, Lark thought. She folded her arms around her as she waited for the rain to subside long enough to make out the street names to somewhere that she could seek shelter. As she stood there, one of the vehicles that was passing began slowing down, and immediately Lark's guard was up. Her muscles tensed as she waited for yet another nasty insult. Much to her surprise, the passenger window rolled down, exposing a woman's hand, which protruded out in spite of the weather, and a shrill voice beckoned her to listen. "Sweetheart, are you OK? Do you need a ride somewhere?"

Lark's ears perked up at the opportunity to get to a drier and more comfortable setting. They seemed like a normal couple, but Lark was still leery, and despite her need, remained hesitant. "I'm not in the habit of being a hitchhiker."

"And we aren't in the habit of picking them up either, at least not these days, but you look like a stray. There's a coffee shop about two miles ahead if you care to go with us. We are visiting our daughter from college, and she asked us to meet her there." The woman's face was kind, and Lark felt her guard drop a little as she told them "OK" and that the ride was appreciated.

"Oh, not a problem," the gentleman chimed in. He looked a little older than his female companion, but not by much. Whereas her hair had remained a dark brown color, his was feathered with gray that gave more definition than anything. Both appeared to be in their late forties or early fifties, and, from the look of their car and clothing, were either upper middle class or were pretending to be.

Lark thought it best not to move around too much, as she felt the seat squeaking underneath her due to the drenched clothing, and she wondered if she was making a mess for them after she left their presence. She didn't want to be inconsiderate, but they honestly didn't appear bothered by it to say the least. And as long as they didn't mind, she was happy to go along with the ride. Her nausea had caught her by surprise earlier on, thus allowing her little opportunity to assess herself or her surroundings. She knew that the diner, or whatever it was called, would require money. It was bad enough she had to bum a ride. She couldn't possibly ask them to buy her something there as well. Or at the very least, she didn't want to.

She reached into the pockets of the jacket she was wearing. Nothing but lint at the bottom of them. Next, she wiggled around until she could thrust a hand deep into each of her pant pockets. Still empty—no cash, no coins. Her heart began to race again as she tried to think quickly how she would manage with nothing but literally the proverbial "clothes on her back."

Think, Lark, she told herself, but nothing came to mind. She even reached her hand into the remaining back pockets of the pants but with no results. "Ugh," she muttered under her breath. But she politely kept smiling, not wanting the generous couple to detect her panic.

"So what brings you out on a rainy night in Laudale?" the woman asked, pulling down the visor above the seat and readjusting her makeup.

Lark looked away so as not to make the woman think she was staring at her. "I guess I just needed to get out of the house for a bit. Didn't realize the weather was gonna be this bad. Kinda caught me off-guard," she replied, knowing there was some truth to her comment but anything more would have to be "creatively orchestrated."

"Well," the man chimed in with a hearty laugh, "I'm glad we were there when we were! As you can see, the weather is only going to get worse. You are more than welcome to sit and eat with us if you care to. No obligations. But I'm sure Grace wouldn't mind."

Both of them looked at one another, and Lark bit her lip. She really didn't feel like socializing, but chances were if she did agree, she might be obliged to some hot coffee and a warm meal. Her tummy rumbled now with anticipation as she bantered the idea around in her head. The nausea had passed, leaving her feeling famished, her stomach contents now miles away.

"I really don't want to impose. The ride is enough. But if you are OK with it, then maybe. I don't really talk much to strangers."

"That's OK, we didn't expect you to. We just wouldn't like you sitting all by your lonesome when we can be a help."

Lark held her hands together. Sometimes when she was around strangers, they would shake or fidget a bit, and her nerves would be overactive. "Do you mind me asking what you do?"

"Do you mean for a living?" the man chimed in.

"Yes," Lark said.

"Well, I'm Todd, and this is my wife, Elizabeth. We are missionaries, and we brought our daughter back to the States to get an education here. She wants to be a biologist, and where we were sent, there are no schools or programs for that."

"Oh, I see. That's actually pretty cool. Nice to meet you both. My name is Lark. How old is your daughter?"

Mrs. Elizabeth beamed as she spoke. "She is eighteen. She's a freshman this year, and even though she is young, she is very smart and driven. Takes after her father on that one," she said, turning to Mr. Todd as she spoke.

He smiled sheepishly as if embarrassed by the accolade. But Lark sat back and just listened as Mrs. Elizabeth continued to rave about their only daughter. She wondered if this was the person who needed help, but it didn't appear to be. She seemed like she had the world at her fingertips.

Soon they arrived at a small diner located on the dimly lit corner with a few cars parked in the lot, all as close to the entrance as possible to avoid the rain.

Mr. Todd parked the vehicle as Mrs. Elizabeth grabbed an umbrella and her purse. Mr. Todd walked around the car and opened the door for his wife, a gesture that did not go unnoticed by Lark, as he also opened the door for her. He didn't look anything like her father, but his mannerisms reminded her of him.

"Hurry, ladies," he said as both of them exited and walked inside while he shut the doors behind them.

The diner was warm and dry, and Lark smiled at the waitresses in appreciation. She motioned to Mrs. Elizabeth that she was going to the restroom to wash up and headed toward it. She just wanted to tidy herself up a bit and clean her face off. Her hands still smelled disgusting. At the sink, she began pumping the soap onto them, lathering and shoving them under the running water. Her eyes looked upward at the mirror and stared yet again at the face of a woman who seemed foreign to her. She then dried her hands off with the plain, brown towels from the dispenser and brushed her hair as usual away from her face. She then dabbed another paper towel across her face to capture any remaining drops of water and straightened her clothes into a presentable fashion. She was about to walk out of the bathroom, but as she did, she heard the loud squeaks of her wet shoes and grabbed another couple of towels in frustration to dry off her soles and walk back out in the hopes it wouldn't be so noticeable.

"Lark, we are over here," Mrs. Elizabeth said loudly, her hand in the air. Lark immediately turned a few shades of red but said nothing, more embarrassed than anything, as other diners turned around in their chairs or booths to take a look at the reason for the commotion.

"Yeah, OK," Lark said quietly as she sat down. "Thanks."

Mrs. Elizabeth smiled as she and her husband introduced Lark to their daughter, Grace. Grace was even more beautiful than her mother described. A vision of beauty, truly striking, and eyes so green you stopped to take notice. *More like a model,* Lark thought as she took a seat next to her, feeling a little intimidated for some strange reason, and very inadequate.

"So Mom and Dad have been telling me about you. Lark, right?" she said, turning toward her with gleaming and perfectly straight teeth. Lark felt the anxiety growing as she forced a few pleasantries from her lips and hoped the waitress would hurry up to take their orders.

Grace eyed her but smiled and continued to steer the conversation instead toward herself. "Perfect," Lark muttered and stared at the menu.

The conversation continued as the orders were placed and everyone sat with their preferred drinks, listening to Grace relive days so far on the campus, life in the dorms, and how her professors are. "All of them are extremely nice to me, Dad," Grace said and thrust her upper body forward, flipping her hair around for effect.

"I bet they are," Lark said smugly, instantly feeling guilty that her own insecurities had made her feel that way. It was wrong, and she knew it. She didn't even know this girl and already she was hurling invisible darts her way. Scolding herself, she looked up and managed a smile.

"That's awesome," Lark said, trying to sound convincing.

"I think so. If I hunker down, I can ace these midterms and keep that GPA high."

"What is your GPA?" Lark asked curiously. "And how many of your professors are guys?"

Grace looked at Lark as well as her parents, a bit confused by the question. "I have a 3.8, but I'm working toward a 4.0." Her face still beamed. "And I'm not sure what the gender of my professors has to do with anything, but only one is male, if it makes a difference."

Lark felt like melting into her seat. Everyone's eyes boring into her and making her feel like a total jerk. "Ugh, I detest myself," she said under her breath, agreeing to be nice from now on.

Grace Opens Up

No one made too much fuss over Lark's comments, and she was relieved. In fact, as the conversation continued after the meal and into dessert, it reminded her of how she had watched Joseph and his family—that is, before his world was turned upside down. *You aren't gonna do the same thing to me are you, God?* she thought as she fumbled with her hands under the table, a nervous twitch she had never stopped even as an adult.

The waiter was polite and prompt, and while almost an hour went by, it seemed as if they had only sat down. "Thank you for your service, it was excellent," Mr. Todd said.

Lark watched him grab the ticket and pull out his wallet. "Whew, that was a close one," she said under her breath, hoping that, if worse came to worst, she would simply dishwash her way out of a debt.

"No, thank *you*, sir. It was a pleasure," the waiter said after he gave Todd his change.

"You know what, you keep it, Son. You earned it."

"Really? Most appreciated."

"Tell me something," Mr. Todd said as the boy turned to leave. The instant smile soon developed into a frown, as he thought he was about to return the generous tip as if it had all been a cruel joke or maybe due to an absent-minded gesture. Lark held her breath, trying to read the impression on Mr. Todd's face, though both his wife and daughter didn't appear to skip a beat in their conversation.

"Yesss . . . sir?" the waiter responded, prepared to retrieve the money from his pocket.

Noticing the boy's hand moving toward his pocket, Todd said, "No, no, no . . . put that back."

The boy's relief was instant and a little too obvious, causing his face to redden a bit.

"I just wanted to ask you if you needed prayer."

"Prayer?" the boy said, shaking his head. "I don't need that. But thank you."

"Oh, OK. I was sure you did. But all right then."

As the waiter turned to leave, he took a step back and turned about. Lark was stunned and confused, but despite his initial denial, he returned, asking for prayer on his midterm exams. They prayed aloud right then while the waiter stood at the table and bowed his head. Grace smiled, and he returned her gaze. Lark caught it but quietly kept it to herself. Although she had never experienced such, it was something that warmed her heart and made her recognize just how precious and yet how strong the human bond could be if only given the slightest glimmer of hope.

Mr. Todd whispered something in his wife's ear, and Lark looked up to see them both staring at her.

"What's the matter?" Lark asked, feeling self-conscious.

"Nothing, really, we were wondering if there was somewhere else you needed us to bring you since we are about to leave."

Grace smiled. "It's cool, Mom. I can bring her wherever she needs to go. I'm more familiar than you are about this town. It's no problem. Besides, it's still drizzling outside. You guys head to the hotel. I mean, if that's OK with Lark." Grace looked from her parents to Lark.

Lark began to feel uncomfortable. "I was really just thinking about sitting here for a bit. It's nice and dry, and I could use a moment to just rest."

Grace looked worried, as did her parents, but Lark tried her best to assure them that she was just fine and appreciated everything.

"I really don't wanna leave ya here. Do you mind if we just girl chat?" Grace said with enthusiasm.

Lark shrugged her shoulders, but acknowledged it was all right.

Grace's parents said their good-byes and extended a business card with their contact information to Lark after they prayed and left the diner. They were a very kind family, and Lark was truly glad. But "girl chat"? No, that wasn't gonna work, so how to get by herself again? Grace didn't seem to be too perturbed, instead sitting back down in the booth while their previous waiter looked confused.

"It's cool, we just wanted to chat some more. Two coffees please. You do drink coffee, right?" Her gaze now on Lark instead of the waiter she had batted her eyelashes to earlier.

"Yep, sure do. I kinda didn't bring any cash with me though."

"Oh, that's all good, I got it. Just figured we could get out of the earshot of parents for a bit and just talk about life, guys, clothes, you know . . . that kinda stuff."

"Um . . . not really," Lark replied.

"Not really, as in, you don't wanna talk about it, or do you wanna talk about something else?"

"What if I told you that I didn't wanna talk about anything, then what?" Lark said, slowly trying to gauge Grace's expression.

Grace bit her lip for a second, shrugged a bit, and then said they would then just have to drink coffee and stare at each other the entire time. "Sounds kinda boring to me," she ended with a huff.

"I dunno, maybe. Sometimes I wind up having the best idea or a solution to a problem when I am quiet," Lark said, sipping her coffee. Grace was studying her, and she could feel it. One gulp down from an onslaught of questions like Joseph's family had been, but they never materialized.

Grace didn't skip a beat after a moment of silence and began telling her how things really were in her dorm room, the kind of things she didn't want her parents to know.

"Are you saying you have been with guys in your dorm room?" Lark asked, looking up from the final sip of coffee.

"No, I didn't say that at all! What I said is that they, the guys, do try at all hours of the night and that a lot of girls sneak them in, and at that point . . . I don't need to go any further. In fact, I know of some of these girls myself 'cause I have classes with them. But I've always said no."

"Good for you," Lark said, "and I mean that seriously. But what have you done to report what's going on?"

"Well, I went and told the dean, and it just got bad after that."

"Huh?" Lark said a bit confused. "I'm not following you."

"The girls found out about it, and because I took such a stance about the matter, they have purposely bullied me in the dorm and, as of recently, all over campus. I wanted to go home, but my parents have done everything to let me be here and get the education I really wanted. The only way they would get the tuition money back is if something happens to me while I'm attending school. If I drop out, it's gone, and so are my chances of going to another college as prestigious as this one. I just come across looking like a quitter . . . a failure."

Lark took a deep breath. She motioned for the waiter to bring a refill on the coffees, as both of them were out and still holding their cups.

"Yeah, that does sound pretty bad, but these girls are a little too old to be bullies, am I right? OK, go with me for a second. I am not and will never condone bullying ever, but in grade school, we had a few, and we just simply chalked it up to middle school and the crud that goes along with it if you stand out, are too poor, too skinny, too fat, or whatever. Nobody liked it, but thankfully by the time we got to high school, we had kinda developed a little more— changed enough to resemble more of our classmates and no longer the oddball, or at least treated like an outcast."

Grace shrugged as Lark finished speaking.

"Well, did you speak to the dean about it again?" Lark asked, since Grace had simply sipped her coffee, not answering.

"It will only get worse if I do," Grace finally muttered.

"How so? If anything, he would know you aren't about to get pushed around and back off. I don't let people push me around," Lark said inwardly, thinking that sounded rather hollow, knowing she really didn't hang out with anyone in order to have to.

"I dunno. I really wish I could close my eyes, wake up, and it was all just a dream. You know what I mean?"

"Yep, I sure do," Lark said, beginning to fidget with her fingers again under the table.

"I am just hoping that some of them will drop out. I know that sounds bad, but I do. I can't help it. I don't know how much more I can take." Grace took a deep breath.

"Hey, you are gonna be just fine. Look at you. You got everything going for you. Have you talked about it with your parents? They seem really cool. Maybe there is something they could do," Lark responded, trying to be helpful.

"My parents? Are you kidding? No way! They don't need to be bothered by anything."

"Goodness, no need to get irritated," Lark said, quickly holding her hands up at such aggression. Lark watched the redness start to dissipate from Grace's face and a calmness return to her demeanor. "OK, guess we ruled that out . . . though I don't know why," Lark said, with obvious sarcasm.

"I just don't want them involved, that's all there is to it. They've done enough for me right now, and if I can get past these tests and take some time to go home and rest, maybe I can get my nerves in check instead of walking around frazzled all the time."

"So I got to ask, how do they even bully you? Are we talking about grade-school antics?"

"Oh no, they're better than that and much cleverer. It's mainly on the internet and in between classes. I tried to move out of the dorms to get off campus as far as living arrangements were concerned, but when I went to apply, I was turned down at almost every place I went. When I finally got frustrated enough, I asked a couple of them why I had been turned down. My references were impeccable. I had good credit and money to pay them. I don't even own any pets and live very minimally. You can't imagine their responses."

"What?" Lark said, realizing she had actually become concerned and fully engaged in the conversation. Only a mere hour ago she had debated on going to the bathroom until Grace got the hint she wanted to be left alone, and then she would leave.

Grace leaned in closer. "They didn't want 'my kind' living there," she said, slowly making a gesture for quotes with her fingers.

"What does that mean, 'your *kind*?'" Lark asked, totally confused.

"I don't have the foggiest idea. I tried to probe for further answers, but it was like talking to stone walls. Like they had made their minds up before I even showed up. Not running my credit or discussing my means of payment . . . absolutely nothing. I actually get the feeling they felt like they were doing me a favor to even shake my hand. It was creepy . . . like loathing. But that Friday as I was getting back to my dorm room from my last class for the day, there was a sign plastered on my door that said, 'Guess you are here to stay.'"

Grace continued, retelling with a fire in her eyes. "Now I was angry, mind you. I tore it off my door and went into my room to look around, but after a few minutes, I felt like I was being paranoid, and I laid down. But I just couldn't shake the feeling that they were completely responsible for what happened with the 'house hunt.' I still don't know to this day what they said, but if they aren't hacking into my accounts online and telling me horrible things, they are finding anything and everything to make my life a living hell here. I feel watched all the time. Scared to even take a shower in the dorm for fear it's gonna be plastered for the whole world to see. For weeks, I put up with it and just watched my back a little closer, but if they are trying to make me go crazy a little more each day, it's working. I put on a good front for my parents and my teachers, but I'm really not OK. I don't want to give these girls the satisfaction of seeing me come unhinged, but I just don't see much in the form of solutions anymore."

Grace continued. "They never use the same accounts to mess with mine, and even when I changed mine in the past, it only lasted for about three days, and then I had a note, like a screen saver, that said: 'Go kill yourself.'"

"*What*? I would have taken a picture of it right then and there and brought it to the authorities' attention!" Lark said angrily.

"Really, and who you gonna prove put it there? And what if you can't implicate all of them and some are out and about to exact vengeance on you? You aren't me, and you aren't in my shoes. Until then, thanks but no thanks."

"OK, that's two for two," Lark said, throwing her hands up dramatically. "No parental involvement and no law and legal action. Well, I honestly haven't an answer then for you—basically no ideas except you going at them like in an old Western. But that's just silly."

"Yep, I just feel like no matter where I turn, it's gonna be bad. Wish I could just take myself out of the equation." Grace slumped her shoulders and reached for the coffee cup to drink some more, but she was already finished with her second serving and looked disgruntled at its emptiness.

"Why don't you just take a breather, OK?" Lark chimed in and motioned for the check. "Another cup of coffee really isn't gonna help that much, and the last thing you need to do is to jitter back to the dorm room."

Grace went on as Lark gently prompted her to continue with her further incidents. Some trivial, others actually quite frightening, and in some cases even life threatening. The more Lark heard, the more she was convinced that if she didn't intervene, things were only gonna get worse. But if she was there to save Grace, how was she gonna guard her or keep her from danger if she had no means to have a twenty-four-hour watch on her? Grace had to go back to the dorm room where Lark was not allowed, because she was not a student. Lark's only two options were to continue sitting in a coffee shop all night or figure out how to convince her to tell her parents and those who could intervene more than she ever could.

Shaking her head, Lark noticed that Grace had continued to ramble and still not paid the check. Another wave of panic washed over her, but Grace must have read the expression on her face, for within mere minutes, she grabbed the ticket and the holder it sat in, placed a shiny silver card in it, and motioned for the waiter to retrieve it. "What, you thought I wasn't going to pay like I said?" Grace said, chuckling a bit.

"Well, kinda, for a second, but I apologize for it. I was just serious about not having a single bit of cash on me, and I really would feel humiliated if I had been forced as a temporary dishwasher."

"You know they don't allow you to do stuff like that anymore, right?" Grace said, eyeballing Lark closely.

"Huh?" Lark said. "Why not?"

"I don't have any idea. But nowadays, they just call the cops on you unless you get some sort of leniency from the restaurant owner, but I wouldn't count on it. How come you were out walking around in the rain anyway, and without cash? Are you homeless? Don't lie to me either. You either are or you are real close . . . I can tell."

Lark put her head down, pondering how to best answer without admitting that actually she didn't have a clue what it felt like to be penniless or any idea where she was going to go. But the night was still young, and she had always prided herself on quick thinking. "I got a place. Just walked out without any funds," she said matter-of-factly, though "transported" was more like it.

"Oh, OK," Grace said. "I thought for a little while you were just saying that in front of my parents because you were embarrassed. I didn't want to call you out in front of them. Doesn't really matter too much to me in case you just wanted to save face."

"I'm doing OK," Lark said, "but thanks for the concern. Really, I'm not just saying that. I don't have many friends. Don't let these bullies get to you. They only do that because someone did that to them or because they are just insecure and use this as a tactic to feel in control."

"Yeah, I've heard of that before. And even though it rings true, it doesn't change the fact that it still hurts, whether I want to admit it or not, and I just want it to stop once and for all." Grace slammed her fist on the table to reiterate her words, and Lark felt a chill run down her spine.

"I think, if you want, I'd be willing to go with you to talk to the authorities and, if you needed, stick around to talk to you if you care to." Lark was running out of ideas, and the night was just getting later and later with really no clear solution to their problems. The restaurant was not open twenty-four hours, and finding a suitable place to sleep would have to be decided quickly.

"Well, I guess you are right," Grace said after a long pause. "I probably do need to be heading back. But I don't mind dropping you off where you live if you want."

Lark fidgeted her fingers under the table again, her mind racing as she tried to ascertain the best response. "No," she said, "it's fine.

Sometimes it really does me a world of good to keep walking. Helps me sort stuff out, you know what I mean?"

"Yeah, I guess so. Just thought I'd ask." Grace smiled and began to get out of her chair and stand up.

Lark went to extend her hand, but the clanking of the entry door and sudden gust of air caused Grace to look in that direction. In a split second, Lark noticed Grace's face contort to one of fear and her legs shake as if they were about to buckle. Confused, Lark directed her eyes in the direction Grace was staring. As the entrance door finished swinging shut, five girls stood huddled together, whispering as if nothing could be done without a consensus. They seemed to be staring intently in the direction of Grace and Lark.

"Whoa, are those the girls who are bullying you, Grace?" Lark asked, concerned.

"Y-e-sss," Grace said slowly. She gripped the edge of the table, her knuckles white in color. "I . . . think . . . I'm . . . gonna . . . go to the restroom," she stuttered.

Lark simply nodded.

The girls seemed to find amusement at Grace's obvious discomfort and motioned to sit at a table not that far from Grace and Lark's. Giggles and sneers were about the only sounds coming from their table, but it disgusted Lark and bothered her that people could be so cruel for absolutely nothing. Most of them were very pretty and no doubt from wealthier families. *What a shame to resort to such childish and vindictive behavior,* Lark thought.

Lark stared back at them, though her normal tendency was to shy away from people and situations. But this was different. This wasn't just about her. Grace was truly scared. She had seen it in her eyes and felt it in the air as she had watched her dash into the bathroom, visibly upset.

For a few moments, Lark continued to listen as they flippantly yelled at one of the waitresses and brushed the trash from off their table to the floor. It didn't matter to them that the workers were tired and doing their best or that other families and couples had walked in and were also trying to place their orders. The blatant disrespect and lack of decency made Lark angry, but she sat motionless, waiting for Grace to return.

However, minute after minute passed, and Lark began to feel worried and wonder why it was taking so long. Did Grace plan to just sit in the stall all evening long? Lark figured if she wasn't to come out soon, it might be best to go get her and remind her that nothing was going to happen . . . at least not on her watch.

Lark would not have trusted leaving a glass of drink—or in this case a cup of coffee—with the likes of those girls, but since everything was empty and Grace had taken her purse with her, she didn't mind getting up from the table and heading after her.

Lark could feel their eyes fixed on her as she headed toward the bathroom, but she didn't care. She wasn't in the mood to deal with their shenanigans, and Grace had been in there for too long.

"Grace? Grace, it's Lark. Are you OK? I don't want to alarm you, so I'm just letting you know that it's me before I walk in. They are still here, but it's OK. No one is gonna mess with you while I'm around, that's for sure."

Only silence greeted her knocks, and that same dread she felt when Joseph hadn't answered came over her. Suddenly, just as she was about to barge in, a small voice said, "Please just leave me alone. I can't take it anymore."

"What do you mean, Grace?" Lark said compassionately, though the door still separated them.

Almost Too Late

I mean I want to be gone and never worry about any of this ever again," Grace whimpered.

Lark closed her eyes. "Please, God . . . please help me as You helped me with Joseph. Give me the words to say." With that, she pushed the door open forcefully, her heart pounding, not knowing what lay behind the entry.

As it swung open, Lark noticed Grace crouched in the corner, tears streaming down her face, a puddle of blood pooling up beside her.

"Oh, my dear God!" Lark shrieked, already beginning to panic. "What have you done?" She noticed the ugly gashes across both of Grace's wrists. She ran out, yelling for the staff to call 911 and then darted back into the bathroom. The commotion drew everyone out of their seats, including the same girls responsible for Grace's drastic behavior.

Lark made it back to the bathroom, recognizing first aid was vital—Grace already beginning to slump down, the tears still flowing. "Oh, Grace . . . *why?*" Lark said, quietly comforting her. She took a couple of rags from one of the waitresses now staring dumbfounded in the hallway and bound Grace's wrists to stifle the blood flow.

At first, Grace resisted, wincing in pain, but ultimately allowed Lark to bind them up, fear mixing with hurt in her eyes.

"Where is your phone?" Lark asked, scrambling now to locate Grace's purse.

"This isn't what I planned. I thought I'd be gone by now and this would be the end of it," Grace said, pointing to the direction of her purse.

Lark kicked the pocketknife away from where Grace had been sitting and emptied the contents of her purse onto the floor, disregarding the mess or the splatters of blood. She reached down to grab the phone and demanded the pin number to get Grace's parents on the phone.

"No, please . . . don't do it, it will devastate my mom," Grace said, pleading with her as she drew a shallow breath. The paramedics now rushed in and pushed Lark to the side.

Lark dusted herself off, knowing they didn't mean to be rude. "Did you think if you died they weren't gonna be devastated?" Lark looked at her incredulously. "What do you think happens to everyone you leave behind? Let me just remind you that their lives don't go on as if you didn't exist. The loss of you diminishes their lives and takes part of them with you. Did you ever think of that?"

Grace continued to whimper as the medics checked her vitals and continued to bind her deep wounds. The towels that Lark had put on her wrists were now on the side of the door, drenched in blood, causing her to shudder and realize she had almost been too late.

The girls, who a mere hour ago thought everything was fun and games, now stared into the bathroom as many others did in sheer horror, realizing they had almost witnessed the needless end of a beautiful life. There were whispers, gasps, and stares as the blood that pooled around Grace now traveled down into the grout lines between the porcelain tiles, staining them a deep crimson.

Grace tried to shield her eyes from the crowd, but Lark knew she could see them, and it was bothering her tremendously. She felt the phone vibrate in her hands. Realizing it was Grace's parents, she quickly swiped her finger over the face of the phone and put it to her ear.

"Grace, hey, hon. It's Mom. Just making sure you got back safe and sound. Dad and I are back at the hotel and resting." Lark was silent.

"Grace? Grace . . . can you hear me? Do you have bad reception? You can hang up and call me back if you need."

"Don't hang up," Lark said, suddenly finding her voice.

"Who is this?" Mrs. Elizabeth said into the receiver, worry now apparent in her voice.

"It's me, Mrs. Elizabeth. It's Lark. I need for you both to come back to the diner right away, please!"

"Oh my, what's going on, Lark? Where's Grace?" Lark could hear Mrs. Elizabeth waking her husband and telling him to get dressed as quickly as possible.

"Mrs. Elizabeth, I'd rather not say over the phone. Can you both please hurry? Grace is OK though; we just need you both to come quickly."

Mrs. Elizabeth wasn't too convinced but hung up the phone as Lark had hoped so that she could get back to the urgent matter of Grace, who now was positioned on the stretcher. The medics picked up their materials and were preparing to take her to whatever hospital was nearest.

"Her parents are on the way. Can you please wait?" Lark said to one of them.

A young woman who appeared to be in her early thirties, her hair twisted in a bun, and a stern look on her face, looked in her direction. "We really need to get her out of here," she said to Lark, her eyes then looking toward the crowd as if to say, "back up."

"I know," Lark said quietly, "but they are here in town visiting their only daughter who is now on that stretcher, and they need to know that she is OK. There can't be that much traffic on a night like this. When I spoke to her mother just a few seconds ago, she indicated they were in a hotel. Please, just a minute or two more." Lark's eyes pleaded along with her voice.

"Are you her family as well?"

"No, ma'am," Lark said, looking at Grace whose beauty remained unmarred, though her mascara and tears had mixed to form a kind of melancholy mask, "but she is my friend."

"I understand that completely, and the sentiment is not going unnoticed. However, unless you are a next of kin, there really isn't much we can discuss with you. Since she is coherent and stable, once she is admitted, they can visit her there."

Lark wanted to persist that they stay, but she knew it was futile. The majority of the crowd had thinned out or at the very least made their way back to their tables to give room for the paramedics to escort Grace out to the waiting ambulance.

"May I at least know where you are taking her?" Lark said, "just in case they pull up right after you leave with her?"

The same paramedic turned to look at Lark. "Mercy Hospital. Do you know where that is?" she continued.

"No," Lark said sadly, "I really don't. I'm not from here either. But I'm sure I can get directions."

"OK, good. It's just a couple of blocks up, on the left at the corner of Willow and Birch. Can't miss it. The signs are easy to see. And . . ." she said after a brief pause, "your friend is gonna be OK. This hospital has an excellent recovery program for suicidal patients." She patted Lark's shoulder and ran to catch the other paramedic who had gotten Grace already out of the hallway and near the entrance of the restaurant.

Lark followed, her eyes like daggers on the cluster of girls who now sat in silence at their table. Grace did not even look in their direction, simply keeping her eyes closed as the procession of the emergency crew was ogled by the crowd, much to her expense.

Lark, on the other hand, wasn't feeling as demure. Anger welled up in her at the reason behind the suicide attempt. As she passed the girls, the urge to blurt out her rage did not go unbridled. She walked up to their table, looking at them directly in their eyes.

"You know something? You don't know me, and I don't really know a lot about each of you. But what I *do* know sickens me! You all have driven this poor girl to try to take her own life, and you should have charges filed against every single one of you. If she had stayed in there a few minutes longer, her blood would have been on your hands. Whether you want to sit here and giggle like it's nothing, I assure you, this is as real as it gets! When her parents come here and know what really precipitated this and *who* precipitated this, then there is gonna be hell to pay!"

Lark walked out into the rain where Grace was being lifted into the ambulance. "Grace, everything is gonna be OK." Lark tried to be strong for the both of them, her own voice faltering despite the angered outburst earlier.

Grace did not say anything but nodded her head and softly squeezed Lark's hand in acknowledgment. Whatever the medics had given her—or perhaps it was the loss of blood—had made her eyes look glossy and her countenance one of distant thoughts, as if she were gazing upon something far away.

Lark wanted to get in the ambulance with her but knew they would never allow it. She still had Grace's phone but put her purse and all its belongings on the stretcher beside her, knowing that at some point she would need them whether for personal comfort or because they would require a copy of her driver's license or similar form of identification once arriving at the medical facility.

Lark pushed back her own disheveled hair and wiped the tears away. Just like Joseph, both instances had seemed to test the very fiber of her being and rip the heart and soul right out of her. She was weary, exhausted, and emotional.

"I wanna go home now, Amiel," she said quietly toward the sky.

Just then, a familiar vehicle pulled up. Mrs. Elizabeth exited the car and barreled her way toward the ambulance as it headed out of the parking lot. "Stop!" she yelled as Mr. Todd waved the medic down.

"Lark, what happened?" Mrs. Elizabeth asked, still in shock, while her husband talked to the medic.

Lark held her shaky hands as she recounted the entire conversation and then the events leading up to the present moment. She studied Mrs. Elizabeth's face, trying to determine if she understood what she was being told and whether or not it was too much for her to hear. At times, Mrs. Elizabeth's hands would wring harder and faster. But at those times, Lark gripped them all the more tightly, trying to steady her until Mr. Todd was able to do so.

After a few more minutes, Lark finally finished, and Grace's father walked up just in time to hold his wife in his arms before her tears became too much and she sobbed unabashedly on his shoulder. Lark didn't know what to say. She knew the gamut of emotions that coursed through them, and she felt helpless just as before.

"Do you want to ride with Grace?" Mr. Todd asked, finally pulling away from his wife—after Lark retold the story to him as quickly as she could. "They are waiting on you."

Grace's mom wiped her face. "Of course," she said, quickly kissing him. "You'll meet us wherever they are taking her?"

"Yes, it's a hospital not far from here," Todd said.

"OK, good. Are you coming with me?" Mrs. Elizabeth said, turning in the direction of Lark.

"Me? I can't. They said I'm not family, and, besides, you both have done enough for me already."

"Sweetheart, you saved our daughter's life. Are you joking? As far as I'm concerned, you *are* family. Come with me. I know my daughter, and she will want to see you when she wakes up and is thinking clearly."

Lark nodded her head and followed Mrs. Elizabeth to the ambulance.

The ride there was difficult. Lark watched Grace's mother stroke her daughter's hair, pray over her, and whisper words of encouragement in her ear. She half expected Amiel to show up and transport her back home, but within a few minutes, they were exiting out of the back of the ambulance and walking through the sliding doors with the initials "ER" written boldly in red.

Lark took a deep breath. Grace had made a few sounds, but her eyes remained closed as her mother held her hand.

"Ma'am, you are gonna have to complete her admission information while we bring her back and allow the physician on duty to operate."

Mrs. Elizabeth seemed stunned for a moment as they continued to wheel Grace back, but the familiar face of her husband was enough for her to regain her composure. She headed for the other side of the waiting room that had a large sign hanging from the ceiling with the word "Admissions" in large black letters. Lark sat down in one of the chairs, not wanting to get in the way of anything, and because her legs felt weak and despondent.

Lark had no idea how long it would be before Grace was out of surgery, but at the very least, she was still alive and with family who loved her. Hopefully, those who had hurt and treated her so badly would make it a point to right their wrongs despite the current situation. *It's never too late to do the right thing*, Lark said to herself, reminded of her father's words when she had been young.

Mr. Todd and Mrs. Elizabeth had now finished answering questions and completing the paperwork. Sitting next to her, they held each other's hands and waited. A small television played a couple of sitcoms, but there was nothing funny about sitting in the emergency room. Lark almost got up to turn it to something else because the laughing on the show felt disrespectful and inappropriate, considering the setting. But she knew it was not up to her, so she closed her eyes to think of other things. She must have dozed off because she felt a hand touch her shoulder, and she almost jumped completely out of her chair.

"What! What's the matter?" she said loudly, still in a dream-like state.

"It's Grace. The doctors have finished, and she is resting in a private room. We can go see her now. We knew you were sleeping, but we didn't want to head to her room and leave you here. Would you like to walk with us?" Mr. Todd said, his hand outstretched to help her stand.

Lark rubbed her eyes and tried to mumble that she did not need the extra help, though she was appreciative, and stood up on her own. She felt as if she had been curled up for an extended period of time and stretched her arms and legs for a moment, smiling sheepishly once she realized it had drawn the attention of everyone in the room.

"Sorry," she said and began walking with Grace's parents down the hall toward the elevator.

After arriving on the fifth floor, they stepped into a dimly lit room where Grace was now resting on a bed. *She looks so fragile*, Lark thought. She hoped that despite all the clatter of their footsteps, she would continue to remain in slumber.

Mrs. Elizabeth must have been pondering the same thoughts, for no sooner had she entered the room than she motioned for her husband to walk a little quieter and lighter so as not to disturb the peacefulness, which seemed more like a divine intervention than a human one.

She looked like a princess. Perfectly still, her hair neatly combed beside her. The rest of her body tucked tightly and warmly under white blankets that smelled of gardenias. At first, Mrs. Elizabeth had paused to look at her, but now she was seated and beckoning Lark and Todd to join her.

"I think we need to pray now," she said in a whisper.

"Now?" Lark said, reasoning that Grace might awake if they did.

"Yes, absolutely," Grace's dad said and extended his hands to hold theirs. Bowing their heads, he began to pray softly for his daughter, for them, and surprisingly for the girls who had teased, bullied, and picked on his only daughter.

Lark started to pull her hand back. The thought of praying for them irked her, and she was taken aback at their prayers of forgiveness instead of justice.

Why don't we pray that they are put in jail? she thought. *That's what they deserve. No chance of bullying anyone else, that's for sure.* She could feel her blood pressure rising as he continued to pray for their hearts to be changed and for his own daughter to also forgive them once she was healthy and able to return to school.

Lark was becoming so uncomfortable she let out a sigh that came out a little louder than anticipated, causing Mr. Todd to pause for a second before resuming. After the prayer, Lark fidgeted in her chair, as was her usual custom, while Grace's parents stood together by Grace's bedside. Lark watched them hold one another and wondered why she couldn't wake up to her parents looking lovingly at her like Grace would, once the medication wore off. She squinted her eyes to stop the tears that were forming. Longing to hold her parents again always brought a flood of emotions and frustrated her now more than anything.

"Are you OK, Lark?" Grace's dad asked as he had gone to sit back down and noticed the grimace on her face.

"I'm all right," Lark said, but as usual it was hollow.

"So why did I feel you tense up in the prayer earlier? Did I say something that upset you or made you feel uncomfortable? If I did, I'm sorry."

"It's OK, I guess. Just . . . why didn't you pray for those girls to be held accountable for what they did to Grace? I mean, aren't you mad about it? I am, and I'm not even related," Lark said unabashedly.

"Oh, trust me, Lark, I am. You have no idea how upset and angry this makes me and her mom. But God will handle that situation. And I'm glad He will because if it were me, after staring at my daughter just now, things wouldn't be pretty. But my job is not to exact vengeance. My job is to be a good representative of Christ, and that means we forgive. It's easy to like the people who are good to us or the ones we personally care about. Anybody can do that! The harder thing is to forgive the ones who don't deserve it, who test your every nerve, and who don't even ask for it or apologize for any wrongdoing. But those are precisely the ones He tells us to forgive." He paused, letting his words sink in and be absorbed in Lark's mind and heart. "Trust me, Lark. This isn't easy; in fact, it's one of the hardest things to do in life . . . if not *the* hardest. But if you don't, it will turn to bitterness and take you down with it. Forgiveness isn't really for them as much as it is for the person doing the forgiving. It basically frees us from resentment, bitterness, and callousness that can creep in afterward and do a real number on our emotions. I'd hate to think there were instances in your life where you didn't forgive and therefore still carry chains that only get heavier with time," he said, eyeing her closely and giving her a moment to speak.

She didn't know if she was allowed to be honest about herself—maybe not about the angel and her reasons for being there, but smaller details, just as long as she was a bit vague. The truth was, she did have resentment, she had held onto anger, and she had not moved on as perhaps she should have after her parents died. Maybe it really was time to let go, but could she?

"Unforgiveness is a trap, Lark. It holds you in on all four sides and doesn't let you move forward in any direction."

Lark thought about his words; they were so simple and yet so profound. Why hadn't somebody just told her that years ago? Perhaps she wouldn't have suffered so long in silence and solitude. Or maybe she was at a point in her life where she could open her heart wide enough to embrace it and bury the hurt and resentment that had only festered for years.

"If there is anything, and I do mean anything, you care to talk about, Mrs. Elizabeth and I are here for you."

Mr. Todd's nonjudgmental and compassionate words touched her deeply, and though she wasn't really ready to share her pain just yet, she could feel it subsiding. She was ready to quit holding on to all the things she could never change and reach out for the ones she could. She knew that Grace's parents sensed there was something more, but that was OK. There was, but once she returned she would seek out the help she needed, and this time, *no excuses*.

Lark had watched two amazing people fail to grasp the beauty of life, even in, and especially in, the toughest of times. Both had so much and yet were so caught up with emotion that all hope had been lost. Is that why God had brought her through time, to remind them that there is always hope? Or did He also do it to remind *her*? Lark sat in silence, still pondering the magnitude of the revelation. All this time, she thought all of this was for them . . . and she was happy to help, never realizing that in His great wisdom and love He had done this on her behalf as well.

Grace was starting to wake up, and Lark redirected her focus to her. She was still very groggy but managed a small smile.

"Mom? Dad?"

"Yes, Grace," they both chimed in unison. "It's us, sweetheart. We love you. How are you feeling?"

Grace looked down for a second, as it was starting to register in her mind that she was in a hospital room. She pulled her wrists up to see large bandages around both of them and cringed. "I'm so sorry, I'm so sorry! I never meant to hurt anybody," she said, whimpering again and sobbing as she still stared at herself.

Grace's dad spoke softly. "It's OK, Grace. None of that matters now. The only thing that does is that we love you, and you are alive and safe. Everything is gonna be OK. We will take it one day at a time, and, most importantly, we will do it together."

Lark looked up just in time to see the now familiar bright light in the hallway.

Going Home

A miel." Lark wanted to scream but refrained. Not quite sure if her outburst would only startle Grace and her family.

Amiel stood regally in the hallway, his wings looking even more massive than their last encounter. Lark expected to simply be whisked away, but he didn't flinch. She knew he could probably read the expression on her face as she wondered why she was still there. *Have I not intervened as God wanted? The girl is OK now, right? So why the delay?* She turned toward Grace and her family, still puzzled.

Was she being given a chance to say good-bye? Why had she not with Joseph and his family? Guess it didn't matter. She knew that perhaps something was still missing or needed to be done here, but what?

She scratched her head and looked back at Amiel. It was impossible to read his facial expressions.

"You know, I think I left something in the hallway," Lark said as Grace and her parents looked up at her pacing a few steps around the room.

As she began to walk toward the door, Grace whispered her name. "Lark?"

"Yes, Grace," Lark said, turning around for a second.

"Thank you for saving me . . . for reminding me that death is not the answer. I don't know how to repay you . . ." her voice trailing off as if she was about to fall asleep again.

"You don't need to thank me, nor repay me, Grace. The greatest thing you can do is live. And not just live, but live to the fullest." Lark paused, trying not to get emotional before leaving.

Grace nodded her understanding and closed her eyes. Lark walked out of the room, and in an instant, the bright light and Amiel's strong voice telling her not to be afraid echoed in her ear.

When she awoke, she was on her bed again, this time feeling even more exhausted than the time before and wondering where her angel friend was this time. Had he stuck around like before, or had he vanished again to be in heaven or elsewhere?

She wished he would tell her things about heaven, but he never did, and it was pointless to keep asking him. Besides, she didn't know if angels were allowed to get angry, and she didn't want to chance it.

Lying down in bed, she looked up at the ceiling and smiled. Even if she were older again, she was so pleased that she had also been able to help Grace, like Joseph. And Mr. Todd had been right: *she had held on to the things that had happened to her parents and the person responsible for far too long.* Maybe that's why she could never stay happy. Why, no matter how many times she attempted to reach out to others, determined to share her life, she would wind up resorting to solitude. The happiness was too short-lived, and her trust in people never lasted very long. Anxiety and depression had been the chains that had bound her, but until she had talked to Grace's dad, she hadn't even fathomed that another chain had bound to her first one and had birthed all the other chains. For so much of her life, a barren wasteland of—dare she say the word—*unforgiveness.*

"Amiel, are you still here?" she called out in the room.

"Yes, Lark. I am here with you."

"Good," Lark said, "because I can't seem to find the strength to get up and see you. For some reason, the last time must have done a number on me, and I don't even want to get out of these blankets."

"It is all right, Lark. You should rest." His voice was soothing and made her feel even more relaxed and sleepy.

"OK, Amiel," she said, yawning. "Don't leave me, though . . . just stay here for a little while longer." Lark's eyelids began to droop, and she smiled at him sleepily.

As she slept, Lark dreamt of angels like Amiel. Hundreds of thousands of them all going in various directions and glorious to behold. They didn't seem to notice her, but just to see them in such an orderly and magnificent fashion was breathtaking. *Is this what heaven is like?* Lark thought, though all she could see were angelic beings. She remembered the stories in Sunday school, but it wasn't anything like this. Maybe she was simply dreaming about them because Amiel had been on her mind as she drifted to sleep.

Amiel . . . he was such a kind angel. Would she see him in heaven one day? The thoughts crossed her mind, and she quickly dismissed them as she pondered just how long the reunion would be and if he'd ever ask her to help someone else again. If he did, she would probably go. In the meantime, she would seek out the man who had not been paying attention to the road the night he collided with her parents, sending them to heaven and leaving her with a vast amount of wealth but a devastated heart. She would have gladly given away every dime to bring them back, but that was not going to happen. She needed to accept that and choose to live in the present with hope for the future. Just like Joseph and Grace. They too felt hopeless, but God had other plans and wanted them to see and know that He did have a plan and that everyone had a purpose. Even if they didn't see it at the time.

Lark's mind continued to contemplate as she rested; all the while, Amiel did not leave. He stood by, watching, waiting. Lark's facial expressions kept changing as she dreamt. She had not yet seen these latest changes, and it pained Amiel that they would be hard to accept. But that's what humans failed to understand. They wanted longevity and questioned why everyone was not granted it. In their minds, it seemed cruel that one person should live to ninety and a child should die before he or she became an adult. However, upon closer examination, one simple truth eluded them—the only thing that served to answer what they failed to ever understand: once the purpose of their existence is over, they could come home. And in some cases, their death brought Him far more glory than even their life could have.

Lark had been granted something Amiel had never witnessed: the opportunity to go back in time and help others see that they still had a purpose, that they had meaning, that they mattered, and that above all, they must not lose hope. For hope, true hope, is found only in the Creator.

He was glad that Lark had chosen well. Though it had cost her physically, it had gone so much further in an amazing way to heal her own hurt. Was that not reward in and of itself? *Why do humans never understand the power of kindness?* Amiel thought. Perhaps in a world so full of pain and devoid of concern, a new wave of difference makers would rise and begin to heal and restore the brokenhearted, to strip away the lies of self-loathing, worthlessness, and hopelessness, to extend ears to listen, hands to help, and arms to hold.

"Will they ever be that brave, Father?" Amiel asked, looking toward the heavens.

"Yes," a voice uttered. "Even now I am speaking to their hearts, preparing them, equipping them, and stirring the chords of compassion. These are the 'brave hearts' whose desires are to alleviate the pain and suffering of the world due to rejection, violence, greed, apathy, fear, jealousy, betrayal, hate, worry, illness, abuse, poverty, and hunger. And while their hearts may be human, they beat with divine strength, for it is in My perfect love that there is existence, purpose, redemption, and restoration for *all* My creation. They see Me when they see love, and when they see love, they have *hope*."

Amiel bowed his head and continued to wait. Unbeknown to this human, Amiel had not only returned to take her back but to take her home. He wondered if she would be delighted by the news or if she would question it. She still slept, though Amiel knew it wouldn't be long. Her recent mission had aged her to the point that her body was beginning to fail her, as expected after such progression in the human state.

It was the real reason she was exhausted, but it was not time to tell her. For now, he would simply wait. Time was of little consequence. However, he had been given permission to tell her what had happened to Joseph and Grace, and he knew it would please her.

He had felt the tension in her heart on more than a few occasions, as she had speculated in the past if the consequence of aging had been justified. Now more than ever, on her deathbed, she needed desperately to hear these words. That she truly made a difference for good.

Lark still slept, but despite a myriad of thoughts, the angels ascending and descending kept returning to the forefront of her mind, and with them, comfort and complete joy that she had never known. It was as if all the pain, anxiety, frustration, and grief no longer resided within her. She hadn't experienced such peace and tranquility.

Suddenly, it seemed as if one of the angels stopped and began moving toward her. She could feel her heart beating faster. As he reached out to touch her arm, she uttered a word aloud, the noise of it waking her up instantly only to find Amiel gazing at her near her bed. Her dreams now over, an abrupt jolt of reality hit her as she stared at him, still startled.

"What happened, Amiel?"

"You were dreaming, Lark. Do not be alarmed. All is well . . . rest."

"Yes, rest," Lark echoed, still yawning and short of breath. She was a little thirsty and did not feel as if she had the strength to stand, much less walk to the kitchen in order to do so.

Amiel saw her and reached out to inquire whether she was all right.

"Never thought I'd say this to an angel of all people, but I am very thirsty. Could you bring me a glass of water? My lips feel so parched." Lark looked up at him earnestly.

"Yes, I can bring you some water," Amiel said, the sound of his wings brushing against the floor as he walked. Within moments, he had returned with a glass half full, but Lark wasn't complaining. She didn't want to be alone and welcomed the fact that he had stayed for so long.

Why? she thought as she went to lift up her arm to grab the glass. But upon seeing herself in its reflection, the glass fell from her hand, crashing to the wooden floor and shattering into pieces by the bed.

Amiel was there no sooner than it had happened. His hand extended to touch hers.

"A-M-I-E-L," she said slowly, as the words seemed difficult to form, "I'm old."

Amiel knew that she was scared. He took his hand and brought it close to her heart. "It's OK, Lark. Be calm and have no fear." His strong hand rested over hers, helping her anxiety subside as her heartbeat began slowing down and breathing became steadier.

"What's gonna happen to me now?" The fear of the unknown tried to resurface, and the look of helplessness and frailty shown in her eyes as she spoke.

Amiel's gaze was one of strength and resolve. He didn't want to say anything too hurriedly that might alarm her. He spread his wings and positioned himself on a bench beside her bed. "This last assignment has aged you considerably. To the point that I have remained to take you home when it is time. I don't wish to alarm you, but work now is finished and your new home—your *real* home—awaits. I have been chosen to guide you there."

"But . . . Amiel . . . I'm scared. Is it going to be painful?" Lark asked, her eyelids fluttering with a mix of confusion and excitement.

"No, Lark. Feel the peace as He can give. There is freedom and sweet release in surrender. Don't let human fear hold your happiness hostage. This is only the beginning of forever."

Lark's breathing was becoming more and more shallow. Her body less and less responsive. She could still think plainly and objectively, but the physical was found wanting. She had very little strength, and every time she tried to move to turn her body left or right, she felt a wave of nausea, forcing her to remain transfixed on her back.

"I feel so weak, Amiel. Surely, there is something you can do to help me. I don't want to just lie here until the end."

Amiel drew closer to her bedside and whispered in her ear. Although the ancient words were unrecognizable to Lark, a calmness consumed her as she had never felt before, and she smiled up at him, still so weak but her spirit renewed.

"Thank you, Amiel, I feel much better."

"You are so welcome, daughter of the King."

"Amiel . . ." Lark said after a moment, "what happened to Joseph and his family as well as Grace and hers? Did they grow up? Are they still safe? I wish I could have seen them after, you know, just to make sure they were all right and happy."

As Lark spoke, she half expected Amiel to keep such things to himself, but after she had finished speaking, a smile arose upon his face and his angelic body seemed to illuminate even more, much to her amazement.

"This I can answer for you, as I know it has weighed heavily on your heart. Joseph is now a minister with three children of his own and a young wife who also walks in the Light. His sister has offspring but by a man who did not serve the Father. At this time, even as we speak, He is grooming and preparing her and her future mate for their encounter and subsequent unity. Joseph's mother and father eventually sought guidance, and Darnell now loves his wife in the appropriate manner, as he was led to Christ Jesus by no other than Joseph himself. All are doing well, Lark. You would be pleased."

"What about Alva?" Lark questioned, thinking for a mere second he might have forgotten to discuss her.

"Alva went home to heaven quite a while back. Though her family still suffers from emotional attachment, she is a citizen there and no longer confined to such worldly concerns or ailments. Now that her purpose has been accomplished, it was a pleasure as well to usher her into the Kingdom."

"You took her?"

"Yes," Amiel said softly. "And now I will take you when it's time."

"I'm so happy to hear that Joseph and his family are OK. When you took me away afterward, I wondered if he had been all right. It was heartbreaking to see him so devastated, but I am oh so pleased that he chose to continue living, and not just living, but flourishing. Still amazes me that he really thought for a time that there wasn't anything worth living for. Does he ever speak to anyone about that night?" Lark asked. She coughed a bit and turned her head toward Amiel.

"Yes," Amiel said after a moment of silence. "Yes, he does. He thinks you were an angel, but despite the inaccuracies, he does give all glory to the Most High for saving him from such despair and grief. He also mentors young adults, specifically those who are at high risk for those types of tendencies. You would be thrilled to see the lives that have been changed all because he made the choice to live and be used to bring about hope and compassion to others who were, and are, hurting for a variety of reasons."

Lark took a breath; they were becoming shorter, but her heart wasn't heavy. Amiel's words breathed life into her, and a sense of fulfillment seemed to consume her entire body.

"Oh, Amiel . . . and what news of Grace?"

"I will tell you that, though her recovery wasn't an easy one, her parents faithfully prayed for her the entire time, and it took a strong commitment on the part of Grace to forgive the girls who bullied her after she was well enough to go home and be trusted to live alone. Many angels surrounded her during this time. Once she began to draw closer in her faith, the healing came, and she is now an advocate against that behavior. Even so much as she gave up her job to speak at a variety of venues. Everything from churches to high schools to television. Her story caught on like fire, and she dedicates all proceeds toward this cause. She is still unmarried, but she finds much joy in being able to travel and go where God leads. Her parents are still leading missions in furtherance of the gospel.

"However, one of the greatest highlights is that recently two of the girls who had bullied her showed up at one of her conferences and publicly accepted the gift of salvation. When she heard their names being called at the end of the conference, she went and wept with them. It was the confirmation that she had longed for, and what a reminder of the Father's love to humanity. She is unaware, but opportunities will continue to open up for her to do even more. She still thinks of you and thanks the Father for you in many of her speeches."

Lark could hardly contain her joy. Finally, she had seen the purpose that, at first, she hadn't or didn't want to recognize. That someone as seemingly insignificant and inconsequential as she could have such an impact.

She recalled a particular instance when a man had come to their community when she was little to speak about hunger and poverty. While those issues were his specific focus, the discussion became more global in its platform. After finishing his speech, he had proposed a very poignant question to his audience: "Have you solved world hunger?"

Much to the crowd's credit, though, they had brought new and fresh ideas to the community when the question was posed. Many put their heads down or simply shook them from side to side, indicating they had not solved world hunger.

How she wished she could go back in time and stand bravely and boldly, now knowing the solution. It would take time, perseverance, and courage, but the answer was elementary. Only one requirement could elicit such success, despite the lies that said it was who you knew or what you had that could make such a difference.

Amiel smiled at the revelation so apparent on Lark's face and, more importantly, in her heart.

"All this time, Amiel," Lark said, taking a deep breath, "I really thought, *What good is my existence? How can I make a difference? Who will even listen to me?* But none of that mattered. God wasn't concerned with that at all. I know now how we *will* change the world, starting in our own hearts, then our homes, our towns, cities, nations, and ultimately the world. It's so simple and yet so perfect. Why didn't I think of it before?" she mused.

Amiel's light became brighter and more pronounced as Lark continued, though she had to pause from time to time between words to catch her breath. It was as if the light seemed to engulf him as it did when he was taking her back in time.

"All that is required is to be willing. Everything else can happen and hinges upon that one truth. It gave my life purpose and meaning. For once, I felt like my life mattered. And not just the humdrum drudgery of normalcy, but stepping up and stepping out for others instead of my own self. Recognizing the beauty and gift we call life. I initially questioned this journey; now I am assured that though it took the very breath from me, it was worth the price to be needed, to have a purpose, to be a . . . *maker of difference.*"

Lark let a tear cascade down her cheek as she softly finished, noticing that Amiel continued to illuminate, thus causing her to squint her eyes, the last of her strength spent in the recent recitation of her heart.

"Yes," Amiel said, extending his hand toward her and lifting it up, "and now it's time to go."

With that, Lark lifted her hand just high enough to reach his and closed her eyes, hoping that others would see, believe, and recognize long after she was gone that it wasn't just that every day was a gift, but every single moment as well.